50 Days of Pleasure

National Bestselling Authors

ANITA L. ROSEBORO
MICHELLE D. RAYFORD

50 Days of Pleasure

National Bestselling Authors

ANITA L. ROSEBORO
MICHELLE D. RAYFORD

◆ DEDICATION ◆

To all the seasoned women searching for real love.

♦ ACKNOWLEDGEMENTS ♦

Anita L. Roseboro

First thank you God, for giving me the gifts to be creative. Naleighna Kai, I am grateful that you considered me to be a part of this project. Thank you to our Beta Readers Debra J. Mitchell, and Kelsie Maxwell.

Michelle Rayford, thanks for coming aboard and adding your brand of flair to this project. We must collaborate again. Tribe, thank you just for being there and being an awesome group of ladies and gentlemen.

Readers thank you for your support. I hope you find the series enjoyable, and it brings you a laugh or two.
Much Love.

Michelle D. Rayford

My new motto for all things literary is "Say yes and figure it out later." It's a reminder to myself to get out of my comfort zone and take advantage of opportunities when presented to me. Such is the case for this story and I'm so glad I stretched my writing muscle to embody these characters.

I would like to thank Naleighna Kai for the vision for this series. My tribe members are always there for assistance with beta reads, late-night conversations, and endless support.

To my girls, I hope my example inspires you to pursue your own dreams.

Chapter 1

"Funny you mention taking responsibility, Dallas." Kim, a reporter for the city's local news station said as she twisted in her seat. "We've recently been approached by a woman who claims she's having your child, and you stopped taking her calls. Where is your responsibility on that score, Dallas?"

The lights in the studio suddenly felt like a thousand blazing suns. Dallas squinted, trying to find his agent, Katie Walsh, among the camera crew and other studio staff.

"What are you talking about?" he managed to get out.

Kim touched a finger to her diamond studded ear, a sign she was getting information from someone in the control booth. She nodded like a bobblehead before leaning closer to Dallas, who sat opposite her on a grey, tufted linen accent chair. "Our sources say you met this woman at a charity event, slept with her, and when you found out she was expecting you ignored her calls."

Dallas cleared his throat. *When did this interview turn into a reality show?* His thoughts traced back to see when things went left.

The interview was scheduled by his agent and publicist. Even though it was the NBA offseason, the city was still celebrating the division championship won by the team and looking forward to next season. Dallas began the interview by recounting the game winning play that clinched the series.

"Now let's talk about you a little bit. You were traded here last season and from all accounts, you've been a model teammate. You've even done some excellent work in the community." Kim's ivory cheeks blushed with excitement.

Dallas thought he knew where this interview was going. He had recently launched his 'Build-a-Champ' initiative, which matched at-risk young boys with mentors and provided them part-time jobs with professional basketball teams.

"Yes, it's important to give back. Especially to the youth. As an athlete, kids look up to me. I don't take that responsibility lightly." Dallas flashed his money-making smile. He had to be a man of his word and talk about his support for the children. Dallas knew firsthand what it was like to not have your father's support in daily activities.

His chest tightened as he shook his head. *What woman was Kim talking about? And although this story was creepily similar to how he met Alicia, there was no truth in it.* "This is a totally false claim. You should be careful trashing my reputation over a rumor."

From the corner of his eye, he spied Katie who was giving an earful to the producer.

Kim turned to the camera. "Seems as if the city's new golden boy has a secret."

"This interview is over." Dallas stood, ripping the microphone from his shirt, knocking over the chairs and causing an artificial plant on the table to wobble. Before he could stalk off the set, Kim called his name and motioned for the cameraman to continue filming.

Kim grabbed his arm. "You can't leave. We're not finished."

Dallas tried to walk around her but was halted by her hand on his arm. He raised both hands in the air, aware of the camera capturing the moment. He couldn't afford even the appearance of getting physical with this woman. "Please move and let me pass."

"What are you going to do?" She pointed a narrow finger in his face and struck a pose like she was auditioning for the next episode of one of those "housewife" shows. "Let the world see that not only do you throw women away like trash. You'll hit them too."

Dallas froze. What's happening?

"Come on," Kim taunted him. "You pretend you're a gentleman, but now that the truth is out you want to hit me, don't you?"

"No, he won't touch you, but I will." Katie created a diversion for him. "Now get the hell out of the way."

Dallas glided around the reporter using his signature move to avoid a defender and score a basket. Right now, his focus was the door.

He marched toward the exit aware of people in the control room looking down at him from their glass-enclosed hub. Employees on the floor avoided eye contact, and a few even turned their backs to him. An audio engineer, a slender woman proudly wearing the team's logo on her baseball cap, tossed the hat at his retreating back. A few minutes ago, these same people were asking for autographs and shaking his hand.

Dallas proceeded toward the door, but his head spun around when he heard Katie say, "Try me," and watched his diminutive agent step in Kim's face before he escaped the building.

Katie caught up with him outside the studio.

"What the hell was that?" Dallas gestured toward the metal door he had just blown through. The red 'Recording' sign was still illuminated.

"It was a mistake, is what it was. For them." Katie's bright blue eyes simmered with rage. She removed her signature owl-rimmed glasses and took a deep breath.

Dallas had known Katie since grammar school. Along with his mother, Katie had believed he would make it to the league from the beginning. She made him a promise back then that she would be his agent. Once he was drafted, she made good on that promise. More experienced agents tried to sign him, but Dallas never regretted giving his classmate a chance. She always had his back, and she could pack a mean punch.

"We're never doing another segment with this station. I told the producer we were only here to talk about the recent win. Personal business was off limits." Katie had her cell out yammering away as they maneuvered past two Ford pickups, a Volkswagen Beetle, and a red BMW with Kimmie on the license plate. "These small local shows are always looking for an angle."

Dallas stopped in front of his Buick. "What was she talking about? What woman is claiming I got her pregnant? Katie, I'm particular about who I sleep with, and the only person who's recently had that privilege is Alicia."

"I've got Liv on it. We'll get the studio to delete that footage. The last thing we need is SportsCenter picking up the story." Katie continued to type on her phone. "We'll craft a statement just in case."

Like herself, Liv had been with Dallas as his publicist handling all media inquiries from the beginning. One handled the front, and the other covered everything else. Dallas had never been linked to any real scandal, and he'd like to keep it that way.

Katie looked up at Dallas. "Are you sure Alicia didn't tell anyone how you two met? Weird that the person came up with the same story."

After Dallas introduced Katie to his new woman, they had shared dinner, and she was in awe at how quickly Alicia assessed Dallas' situation and made sound financial suggestions for his future. The earning potential for an athlete was short-term if they had health-related issues, repeated on-the-court injuries, or happened to be traded before they reached their potential. Dallas intended to prepare for a future where his paycheck didn't depend on shots falling through a net. "No way. Besides, Alicia's from Chicago. She doesn't know anybody here."

Katie adjusted her glasses. "Could be a coincidence. I have someone from my staff tracking this down. When we find out who this woman is, we'll have more answers. But in the meantime, you may need to do some damage control of your own."

On cue, his cell rang. Dallas' favorite girl. His biggest fan since he bounced his first basketball. Mom watched every game and interview from the family home in Dallas, Texas. He couldn't say the same about his father whose attitude toward him bordered on indifference.

After seeing Katie to her car with a promise to follow up with her later, he called his mother back from his SUV.

"Hi Mom."

"How's my champion doing today? Still celebrating?" Anna's wide smile could be felt through the phone line.

There was nothing to celebrate after the debacle of an interview. Judging by her upbeat demeanor, he was grateful she had missed watching the live interview.

"I'm okay. But how are you feeling? What did the doctor say at your check-up?" He hadn't spoken with her since before another follow-up appointment. Her annual physical had returned some abnormal test results.

"The doctor said I'm fine, and they'll rescan in about six months. But we can talk about me later," his mom replied. "How did the interview go?"

Dallas took a deep breath, relieved his anxiety could subside a bit regarding her health. "Well, it wasn't the typical interview. That's all I'll say."

Anna laughed, and it put his mind at ease. "You're always complaining about how reporters ask the same ol' questions. Guess this one threw you for a loop."

"More like pushed me over a cliff." Dallas was glad his mother couldn't see his face. He normally shared most things with his mom, but he didn't want to worry her about this "alleged" pregnant woman. She had warned him on more than one occasion about women trying to trap him because of his status. Some women saw him, and their eyes lit up like a slot machine with a winning spin. Dallas had done his dirt, but he was always careful. He didn't play games with women's hearts, and he would remember a woman he met at a charity event. The only woman who could tell that story was Alicia.

And he knew she wasn't the one coming at him this way. She didn't play those kinds of games.

"Mom, I'm going to Canada for a few days," he said, thinking a trip out of the country would help keep his mind off this situation. Plus give him some time with Alicia. He had a commercial shoot scheduled for next week, but he was sure Katie could have it moved up.

"Why are you going there? Business…or pleasure?"

"A little of both," he said. "Liz scheduled a commercial shoot for the new shoe release. And I'm taking a friend on a getaway."

Anna asked, her voice laced with excitement. "Does this woman have a name? Is this something serious? Why haven't I met her yet?"

Dallas chuckled at the rapid-fire questions. "Hold on, Mom. All I'll say is that she's someone special. Hopefully, you'll meet her soon. But I'm taking things a day at a time with this one."

"Okay, keep me waiting," she teased. "Between you and your sister, one of you will give me grandkids before I'm too old to play with them."

His Mom could be counted on to turn any conversation to her favorite subject, grandchildren.

Dallas eased the car into the driveway outside of the restaurant. He thought his interview would run long and had arranged for Alicia to meet him here. Plus, he needed to be sure the venue was prepared for their visit. "Now I know it's time to go. Talk to you later, Mom. Love you."

Anna laughed. "Love you too, Number One Son."

He ended the call but didn't leave the vehicle right away. He was glad things were good with his mom, but there was another woman he also wanted to make happy. She probably wouldn't be thrilled about some mystery woman claiming to be carrying his child. Their relationship had been intense from the beginning and only about two months old. He didn't want to give her a reason to leave.

Dallas found it hard to believe the woman currently in his home would be the very one he met at a charity auction of all places. One, his mother strong armed him into attending.

This impromptu trip to Ontario, Canada couldn't have happened at a more perfect time. He could whisk her away while this craziness was worked out by his team. A change of scenery would be good for them. He sensed Alicia getting restless and wanted to prolong their days together. Since her husband passed away, Alicia was determined to fulfill her lifelong dream to travel. They'd already shared a few trips, and he knew it wouldn't take much convincing to get Alicia to pack her bags again.

Dallas shook off the ambush of an interview and stretched his long legs outside of the vehicle. The thought of seeing Alicia relaxed his shoulders and put him in a better mood. There were two things he knew for certain as he handed the keys to the valet. He was falling in love with Alicia. And there was no way he was telling her about any of this.

Chapter 2

This can't be real.

Alicia had lost count of the times she said this phrase to herself. Her time with Dallas Avery was a real-life fairy tale she didn't want to end. But like most things in her life, she knew it would. *It's only a matter of time.*

For now, she was going to enjoy the moment with this man. Tonight, he requested her presence at Reunion Tower. She had seen the recognizable landmark located in downtown Dallas but had never taken a tour inside. The observation deck boasted the best panoramic views of the city.

Alicia moved from the bathroom into the master bedroom, amazed at how comfortable she felt in Dallas' tri-level condo. They'd only known each other for a short period of time, and most of those days were spent traveling for one reason or another. A lucky draw brought them together.

* * *

Paul Alexander Foundation Charity Auction

"Thank you for your patience!" The strawberry blond host crowed to the expectant crowd who had waited through double overtime for Dallas Avery to arrive. "Folks, our grand prize bachelor is in the house. So, let's get this done. Hearty applause rang out as she reached into the envelope and pulled out a slip of paper. "And the winner for dinner— oh, that rhymed," she said with a laugh and unfolded the sheet. "Is ... Alicia Mitchell from Chicago, Illinois."

Dallas, clad in a black tux, left the stage amid a weak smattering of unenthusiastic applause. He walked past several crestfallen women who had also put in a silent bid to have dinner with him.

All she wanted was an autograph from the NBA champion, even though she was a Chicago Bulls fan. But Dallas insisted on fulfilling the full prize she'd won with a contribution to the charity. Conversation at dinner led to a trip back to his place. The first time shouldn't have happened, but she absolutely had no regrets. Experiencing her first orgasm after a 26-year marriage, made her agree to "just one more day" which was Dallas' favorite question at the end of each night.

These days could soon come to an end if she followed up on the proposal she received today. She had yet to share it with Dallas. Maybe she would inform him at dinner.

Glancing at the card Dallas left for her this morning, she wasn't sure if she would be able to tell him anything. He had left for his daily workout with a kiss on her lips and instructions to pamper herself while he was gone.

"The off-season doesn't mean you stop working on your game," Dallas explained. "The players who make it to the top and stay there work harder than the next guy. This season taught me I have to keep grinding. It shouldn't take us another five years to get a championship."

Watching his dark brown eyes dance with excitement while he talked about plays, angles on defense, and the camaraderie of the guys made her wish for the sense of belonging that seemed to allude her. Alicia's family consisted of her brother, niece, and an evil sister-in-law who was slimier than a snake and only cared about taking what Alicia had for her own. Her parents and twin sister died while she was young. A childhood spent longing for stability led to a loveless marriage with a guardian who locked her down before she realized she had the choice to say no. Once her husband passed, Alicia was left with a hefty inheritance and time to figure out her next phase of life.

The trip to Texas was only scheduled to last two days. It's been fifty sunsets, and she'd enjoyed every moment with this man. But maybe it was time to end this wonderful phase in her life and move on. Before things went bad, as they tend to do with her in matters of love.

Shaking off the feelings of unworthiness that threatened to dampen her mood, Alicia picked up the card Dallas left on her pillow before leaving this morning. She had lingered in bed cocooned in the scent of his essence until hunger drove her out of the sheets and down to the kitchen. The rest of the day was spent overseeing the renovations to the recently purchased but unfurnished home. Alicia basked in the task of procuring furniture and decorations for his space. She couldn't wait until he laid eyes on the mahogany desk delivered today for his home office.

A loud chirping noise pulled her from her work. The cell phone displayed his name, and her lips parted at the thought of him.

"Are you getting ready for me, baby?" Dallas' deep melodic voice sent a tremor through her ear straight to her core. This connection between them was so intense, at times Alicia could almost see the simmering chemistry when they touched. The bond scared her if she focused on it too long.

"You've been gone all day," she teased. "This evening better be good. You're making me dress up and everything."

Alicia put the phone on speaker and returned to the bathroom. She applied the fragrance of vanilla and lavender that he loved in all the right spots to assure his appreciation.

"Thought we could use a change of scenery. Get out of the house."

Alicia wasn't objecting to the amount of time spent inside the sanctuary of his home. His imagination didn't lack for activities to keep them busy. Her mind wandered back to last night when he had pulled out a jar of habanero honey and poured it on her breast. The tingle from the peppers on her nipples was divine. She could still feel the aftershocks and would for days.

"The driver will be there soon," Dallas said. "I'll be waiting." He gave her the name of his regular driver along with sending a picture.

Little things like that, the attention to detail, only made him dearer to her heart.

At approximately half past six, a black Lincoln SUV pulled up. Three soft taps on the door happened at the same time as she swept her cape off the sofa. She peered through the peephole and saw an older gentleman in a tux.

"Ma'am, I'm Greg your driver for the evening. Mr. Avery gave me strict instructions to deliver you safely to him tonight."

Greg looked exactly like his photo. Salt and pepper hair and a bushy mustache. She set the alarm, grabbed her purse, closed, and made quick work of locking the door. Alicia took the arm extended to her as Greg escorted her along the brick pathway to the car. Once she was settled, he pulled off.

She settled comfortably in the supple leather seats, taking in as much of the scenery as she could in the dark night. Several street signs and buildings later, she was able to make out the Dallas convention center and knew they were close.

Greg pulled into the Hyatt Regency parking lot. As the car rounded the drive, she could make out a lone figure standing at the entrance.

Dallas.

Alicia was almost frightened by the way her body reacted at the mere sight of this man. The car barely came to a stop before Dallas opened the door. The scent of his familiar fragrance hit her, and she welcomed his embrace, her body flush with his.

She craved him like a sunflower searched for the sun. One smoldering look or simple touch, and she was a willing vessel, open, ready to receive his love and a lot more. Alicia didn't know how long they stood there, lost in each other. Their lips met, and tongues did a dance as the now familiar rhythm caused them to sway together.

Alicia didn't miss the low growl that passed through his lips as those smooth hands glided down her back and ended on her hips. Breathless, she said, "Did you miss me?"

"Indeed." Dallas deepened the kiss between them. He nibbled on the space right below her ear, sending shockwaves that weakened her knees. Dallas tightened his hold, and she leaned one leg between his.

Alicia smiled and opened her eyes to see the driver had disappeared. They also had attracted some attention from a few pedestrians on the walkway. "Maybe we should take this show inside." She stood on her toes to whisper in his ear.

Dallas took a beat to recover, but he adjusted his clothes and nodded. "Come, follow me."

Looking upward, Alicia took in the expanse of the tower. The adjacent Hyatt Regency Hotel was dwarfed by four shafts of concrete which comprised a building with a three-story globe on top. The lights illuminating the night sky twinkled in competition with the stars.

Their footsteps echoed across the marble floor while entering the center with an empty security desk set on one side and a bank of elevators on the other. The center counter displayed signs for ticket purchases but lacked anyone working behind the desk.

"The place is considerably empty for this time of night." She glanced at Dallas as they continued toward the bank of elevators.

"It would be packed if I hadn't bought out the restaurant for the night." Dallas winked. "I want you all to myself."

Alicia almost missed a step.

A grey-haired gentleman in a white security shirt returned to the desk and waved them past the ticket scanner. He swiped a badge and pressed the call button for the elevator. "Thanks for bringing excitement back to the city, young man," he said.

A casualty of going out around town was the many sports fans who wanted to show appreciation to their favorite new player. Dallas Avery had brought his championship pedigree to this town and with it came a new level of fame. Alicia was familiar with being overlooked by his fans. Dallas handled the attention well. But tonight, he had made sure they wouldn't be interrupted, and she was grateful.

The glass-enclosed car provided breathtaking views of the city as they ascended 560 feet into the air. The heat from Dallas' piercing dark brown eyes singed every part of her body it touched. She forgot about the everything else and took in the marvel of a man. He wore an Italian-cut black suit tailored to his chiseled, muscular frame. A crisp white shirt was open at the collar, and his facial hair was neatly trimmed.

Dallas smiled and continued to stare.

"What?" she asked.

"Do you like what you see?" He struck a pose, head held high with one hand in his pocket. A cover model would not have been more perfect.

Alicia placed a hand on her chest and pretended to swoon. "Someone thinks he's all that."

"No, I'm not. But you are." Dallas closed the space between them and kissed her forehead. "Did I tell you how amazing you look tonight?"

She felt exposed to him. Not that he hadn't seen all her physical form, but now she felt he was seeing her soul. This feeling frightened her. Alicia felt "seen" by him. And if he could truly see her in every way, wouldn't he eventually grow tired of her too?

"Dallas, I …" Those were the only words that slipped past her lips as the chiming of the elevator signaled they had reached their destination.

His eyebrow raised in a question, but she shook her head. Dallas laced his fingers with hers and led her to the observation deck. Together they stared at the city. The towering landscape was breathtaking.

"I've lived here all my life and have never been here before. My teammates told me this was a great spot to take a special lady. They weren't wrong," Dallas said.

"Are you calling me special?" Alicia teased. She removed the shawl, revealing her bare shoulder. She heard his intake of breath right before he said, "Damn." Her backless dress, a royal blue asymmetrical number, with a kick split that ran all the way up the right side of her "see no evil".

Dallas swallowed hard and looked at her with lust in his eyes and desire on his lips, "You are gorgeous. I'm the luckiest man in the world."

Alicia placed a hand on his chest. A piece of her armored heart melted from the heat between them. "Dallas," she said in a whispered breath.

He closed the distance between them. "We started with dinner, remember?"

Oh yes, she remembered.

Her first ever one-night stand had turned into a lengthy affair. Dallas was a fantasy come to life. One of the NBA's most eligible bachelors seemed to have a talent for making her feel special.

"Let's enjoy dinner, and maybe you'll get lucky tonight." Dallas laughed as he dodged her playful swipe. He kissed her forehead again then turned to escort her inside Five Sixty restaurant.

Celebrity chef Wolfgang Puck's restaurant was enclosed by glass on all sides to allow panoramic views of the city. A mixture of wooden tables and brown sofas were flush against the walls for optimal viewing. The open kitchen permitted patrons the opportunity to watch the master chefs at work preparing world-class dishes.

"Welcome, Mr. Avery," the maître d, a short balding man, greeted them. "I'm Joseph, and I'll make sure you have a wonderful time tonight." He led them to a table set for two. "Everything is set to your specifications."

The lights were dimmed, with candles placed in the middle of the tables providing romantic lighting. Dallas pulled Alicia's chair out, and once she was seated, he took the seat in front of her. A waiter and a waitress, both dressed in black from head to toe, stood at attention along the wall close by.

Joseph swept an arm toward them. "These are two of our best servers. They will make sure your dining experience with us tonight is perfect."

Dallas nodded toward the servers, and Alicia smiled at the gesture. This man was full of surprises. Her late husband would never have been so thoughtful.

Joseph executed a small bow. "I'll check on your entrees." He motioned for the servers to come forward before he retreated to the open kitchen.

"Champagne?" The waitress approached and picked up a bottle that was chilling on the table. "I'm Jessica. I had to fight ten other servers for the chance to meet you," she confessed. "I'm a huge fan, and it will be my pleasure to serve you tonight."

Alicia smiled at the young woman's obvious play for Dallas' attention. Her emphasis on the word 'pleasure' was not subtle.

"Thank you, Jessica." Dallas appeared not to notice when Jessica tossed her long black braids over her shoulder and stuck out her chest. "Could you give us a moment?"

Alicia tried not to smile at the woman's crestfallen expression. Jessica mumbled something but walked over to the empty bar.

The male waiter, who introduced himself as Henry, slid over and ran down the specials for the evening. Alicia allowed Dallas to order for them both.

Once they were alone again, Dallas poured them each a glass. "Here's to you, baby."

"And to you. This is a wonderful way to end the day," Alicia replied and clicked her glass against his.

Dallas took a sip and placed the glass back on the table. Before he could utter another word, Jessica returned.

"Some assorted bread for the table," she said. Steam escaped from the cloth napkin, and Alicia's mouth watered at the smell of freshly baked bread. She reached for the basket but froze at the comment that came out of Jessica's mouth.

"What did you say?" she asked.

Jessica's eyes blinked fast. "I was only telling Mr. Avery that it was so sweet he would buy out the place to take his aunt out on the town. Few guys would want to hang out with family."

Dallas' eyes flashed, but he was able to recover so quickly, Alicia was unsure if she saw the flicker of anger. He displayed the smile that made advertisers want him to sell their products. He reached for Alicia's hand across the table. "You are mistaken," he said calmly. "I've done things to this woman that would get me arrested if we were related."

Jessica's face flushed a crimson color, and she stammered an apology. "S…s…so sorry, but you can't be dating her."

Dallas raised an eyebrow to question that statement. "But I am."

"Now, if you'll excuse us again," Dallas continued. "We'd like to get back to our date."

Jessica pivoted, and her rubber shoes squeaked as she made a dash for the kitchen. Then she paused and tipped back. "Does she know about your other woman? The one that's having your baby. I saw it on the news tonight. We all saw it."

Alicia turned questioning eyes to Dallas. "What is she talking about?"

"I was going to tell you later. I didn't want it to ruin dinner." He reached for her hand, but Alicia pulled back.

Jessica glared at Alicia. "That's right. You're next on his list, lady. All athletes do is hump around. Bet he'll dump your ass, too."

"That's it," Dallas stood beckoning for Joseph. "We no longer need your services." He motioned to the maître d. "Please escort her out of here or we're leaving."

Joseph jumped to attention and wiped perspiration from his forehead. "Yes, sir."

"You're going to pay for this, Dallas Avery," Jessica screamed. She flailed her arms trying to get away, but Joseph and two cooks from the kitchen were able to wrangle her out of the restaurant.

"My apologies for the interruption, Mr. Avery." Joseph wrung his hands. "I can assure you that she no longer works here."

"Thank you." Alicia said, waiting until Joseph left the table.

Dallas shook his shoulders, a habit Alicia observed he did whenever he was trying to reset. The romantic mood at the table was gone. She waited for him to explain about this 'other woman'.

"My interview turned into a shitshow," Dallas began. He explained what happened with the reporter airing an unsubstantiated rumor. He assured her it was false. "My agent is working on it. We'll find out what this person wants and deal with it. You have to trust me, baby. The only woman who could possibly be carrying my baby is you."

Alicia studied the man sitting across from her. Their relationship began with heated passion, and it only burned brighter. Trust was still something to work through, but based on the past month or so, he hadn't given her a reason to doubt him. She wouldn't start now. Now, the age difference between her and Dallas had been the source of contention between them. At least it was for her. Dallas had no such reservations. Children. That was another thing. Both were reasons why she needed to end this so-called relationship. What would happen when more of the public found out?

Dallas studied Alicia, and she avoided looking him in the eyes.

"You know, I wanted to talk to you about my plans," she said. "It's time for me to return home to Chicago. Your house is almost done. The desk for the office arrived today. And after this little fiasco, I'm not ready to be constantly called the old woman you're sleeping with or your aunt."

Alicia had taken on the role of an interior designer since she'd been at his house. Dallas had recently purchased a new place, and to say the home lacked furniture was an understatement. The first night she visited, the man only had a big screen television, a sofa, and a bed. He claimed he was too busy traveling for games to shop for anything.

"I would like for you to stay with me a little longer," Dallas replied. "As for the drama, I can't control crazy fans, but please know I keep my personal business private."

Alicia bit her bottom lip. This thing between them didn't make sense, but a part of her wasn't quite ready to leave him either. But common sense isn't always common. "How much time are we talking? I have to get back to my life eventually." She took a sip of her wine. The cool liquid quenched her thirst much in the same way ice cold lemonade would on a sizzling summer day.

"I want you to be a part of my life," he said. "I'm not ready for this to be over yet."

Just as she started to speak, Henry placed their first course on the table and refilled their glasses.

As soon as the waiter left, she finished her response. "Then I guess

I'll stay for a while." Her cheeks grew warmer as she sipped the last of her drink.

His smile supplied more light to the room then the candles flickering on the table. Dallas poured another round of champagne for them both. Dishes were cleared from the first course as the next was brought to the table.

Watching Dallas lick his lips caused Alicia's mind to wander to this morning's interlude. She had to admit she was beginning to like the new person she was becoming. Being with Dallas allowed her a freedom she didn't realize was missing.

Freedom. Freedom to simply be herself.

"And for dessert, peach sorbet," Dallas said when Henry placed a bowl between them with two spoons.

"My favorite." Alicia quickly moved in to scoop up the icy treat.

Dallas took the spoon from her hand and fed it to her. He took a finger and dabbed a drop from the corner of her mouth. When he sucked his finger, an electric current coursed through her.

Alicia signaled for the check. "I'm ready for you to take me home."

"Where you belong," Dallas added. His intentions were as clear as the glass wall behind their table. Dallas wanted her. All of her. Alicia was looking forward to a sensual filled night. She would worry about leaving tomorrow.

Chapter 3

"NBA Basketball Star Dallas Avery will be visiting Canada to shoot a commercial for a new promo. The Raptors and Mr. Avery also have a groundbreaking and autograph signing at Scalding Community Center."

Noah spun his laptop around and plugged the earphones into Jada's ears. Her eyebrows raised in a questioning gesture looking from the screen back to her friend.

"How does this help me escape?" Jada asked in a barely audible tone to make sure the housekeeper didn't overhear the conversation.

The Soto household was full of workers loyal to her father. School was her break from his rigid rules until her father took her out for homeschooling. Lately, she only felt comfortable in the confines of her bedroom. Noah was the only one allowed in here. Out of all her father's workers, Noah was trusted to be alone with her. He was her closest and only friend.

And he was going to help her get free from her father's grip.

Noah brushed his unruly bangs out of his face and took out the earphones. "This is the answer to your problem." His deep brown eyes searched the entrance and their surroundings as if he suspected the devil to appear.

"He's a good guy. I've followed his career, and he's here to help with the community center. I'm sure he can help with your problem."

"My father took me out of school to keep an eye on me." She rubbed her growing belly. "But I heard him say he was going to get rid of it. He said I'm a disgrace." Jada's eyes filled with tears at her hopeless situation.

Noah lowered his head. He had seen firsthand how ruthless her father could be. Dealing in the Soto line of business, a criminal enterprise fronted by the clean-cut businessman, it was necessary. Mistakes could be deadly. He was disturbed by the way Mr. Tony treated Jada. Now he was risking his life for her to escape her father's clutches. No one deserved to be treated the way she had been.

"Don't worry, I'll have a plan by the time they arrive. I have connections, you know."

Jada scanned her bedroom. Could she really leave the only home she'd ever known? The white wooden rocker in the corner was the place where her mother had read her stories as a little girl. Posters of her favorite boy band adorned the wall and were hung as if they were famous artwork. Even the painted wall was a memory of her mother whose favorite color was pink.

But a recent memory emerged along with the cardigan sweater she wrapped around herself. She could almost hear her mother's voice. *"Your father loves you, but he isn't a good man, J. If something ever happens to me, promise me you'll get somewhere safe."*

Something happened. The worst thing ever happened, and her mother left her all alone. She wouldn't miss this place after all. "What if he finds out you helped me?"

Noah shrugged and folded his arms. "I'll just say you got past me when I went to the bathroom or something."

"He'll kill you," Jada whispered. "I don't want your blood on my hands."

He placed his lighter hand over her much smaller tan one.

"I'm not afraid of dying," he replied with conviction. "I can handle myself."

* * *

"Is that a milk bottle?" Jada gazed at the entrance to the Sterling Inn & Spa Hotel when the car came to a stop in the hotel parking lot.

Noah ran around to help his friend out of the vehicle. "Oh yeah, this building used to be a dairy. Mom says they renovated an old building and made this hotel. It's cool, right?"

"Totally cool."

The sound of rushing waters indicated the proximity to the famous tourist site. Noah knew from hanging out here that they were only about a five-minute walk from Niagara Falls. The good thing about the Sterling Inn was it was situated away from the cheeky attractions and casinos. He doubted they would run into anyone who knew them.

"I've never been here before." Jada spun around in a circle. "Mom talked about going to the Falls one time, but Father wouldn't let us."

Noah took Jada's hand and led her around the building. "We need to go in through the back." He was familiar with the layout since his mom started working here a few years ago.

The three-story stone and concrete building wasn't the biggest hotel around, only forty-one rooms according to his mom, and Noah hoped there would be an empty one where he could stash Jada. The plan was to get her out of her father's house. They would have to figure out what came next.

"Rest here while I scope out the lobby." Noah stopped in the red-carpeted hallway leading to the spa. The soft white leather chairs should keep Jada comfortable while he went to the front desk and tried to find an empty room.

She settled on the sofa and massaged her back. "Hurry, Noah. I'm not feeling too good."

Noah's boots echoed off the marble floors as he rushed through the small lobby. The reception desk was tucked into the wall, and his favorite desk clerk, Marcie, was checking in a couple dressed in typical out-of-town garb, Canada sweatshirts and hats.

"Enjoy your stay, folks," Marcie handed the guests room keys with a smile. Her eyes lit up when she saw Noah leaning against the dark wood column.

"What brings you around here today?" she asked. "I saw your mom head up to the third floor earlier. A guest required extra towels or something."

Noah laughed at Marcie's exaggerated eye roll. "I'll check in with her in a few, but I wanted to see my girlfriend first."

"You know I'm too young for you," she replied and winked.

The ongoing joke between them would probably raise eyebrows if overheard. The gangly teenager and the matronly employee made an unlikely pair.

Marcie unlocked the 'Employees Only' door and moved her ample hips to let him past. "Give me my hug."

Noah stepped into the embrace and inhaled the comforting scent of talc powder and honey.

"Now what mischief are you getting into today? Your mum told me you've been hanging around a new crew of people." Concern knitted her brow, and she crossed her arms.

Noah waved both palms in surrender. "Not me. You know my mom worries too much. I'm just trying to help make ends meet."

Marcie stared at him, and Noah knew if he looked away, she wouldn't believe him. He held her gaze and was relieved when someone approached the desk, giving him a reprieve.

Once she helped the guest, he leaned against the granite counter near her computer. He needed to find out room availability but couldn't see a way to do it without arousing her suspicions.

"Where's Ralph?" Noah scratched his scalp and fiddled with a stranded key card on the desk.

Ralph was the Front Desk Manager and didn't appreciate Noah

hanging around. There were several reasons for the dislike. Noah wasn't an employee. Noah was underage. And Noah may have once referred to the tall, skinny manager as a 'White Steve Urkel'.

"On a smoke break, of course," Marcie said. "Listen, baby. Stay right here for a second. I'm going to run to the restroom. If someone comes, tell them to hang tight."

When opportunity presented itself, Noah struck the keyboard with lighting precision. He had already scoped out Marcie's passcode and scanned the screen to find an empty room. All the rooms in this hotel were different, but there was one that no one particularly wanted. His mom shared that it was the smallest and oddest shaped room. If a guest was unlucky enough to get it, most of the time they requested another.

Noah was in luck. It was empty. He swiftly punched in the code to make two set of keys for the door and minimized the screen. When Marcie returned, he was on the other side of the desk scrolling through his phone.

"Gotta run," Noah said. "Need to check in with Mom. I'll come back by on my way out."

He was down the hall before Marcie could respond.

Jada was in the exact spot he left her, although she was now curled in a ball. If a ball had another ball attached to it anyway. "I don't feel so good," she said and squeezed her eyes shut.

"Got a room for you." Noah helped her up and managed to get her to the hidden room on the first floor.

He helped her to the bed and brought a cup of water that he filled in the bathroom sink. "I'll go find you something to eat. First, I need to check on my mom. I know Marcie probably told her I'm here by now."

Noah was halfway out the door when Jada called after him.

"You better hurry. I think the baby's coming now."

Chapter 4

"Are you a member of the Mile High Club?" Dallas leaned back in the leather chair on the Gulfstream G-IV jet chartered for their excursion to Canada.

"If you're asking if I've ever flown on a private plane before I met you, the answer would be no." Alicia stared wide-eyed at the luxurious cabin and took a deep breath. The air smelled fresher onboard the aircraft, a light touch of citrus and cinnamon.

Dallas watched Alicia explore the plane with a warm feeling spreading through his chest. Like the first time, he knew this would be a treat for her and was pleased to make her happy. He would do anything to keep that smile on her face and happiness shinning from those gorgeous green eyes of hers.

"We'll be ready to take off in a few minutes, Mr. Avery." Timothy, one of the pilots, emerged from the cockpit and began the process of securing the door. His blonde buzz haircut and the severity of the creases in his uniform pants screamed former military. "My brother, Thomas, and I will have you safely to your destination in a three-hour flight time. Please fasten your seatbelts. When we reach cruising altitude, we'll let you know, and you're free to move about the cabin."

"Thank you." Dallas stood to shake the man's hand and grabbed a bowl of red grapes before returning to his seat. Trays of fruits, vegetables, and an assortment of cheeses were set up on a table covered by a white tablecloth. A carafe of water with slices of lemon was stored in a container off to the side. "The twins, Timothy and Thomas, are the best corporate pilots. One of my teammates turned me on to them."

"Have you flown with them before?" Alicia asked. "How many women have you impressed this way, Mr. Avery?"

Dallas thought she was being serious until he caught the sly grin she tried to hide behind a water bottle.

"Only one woman worth impressing."

He watched Alicia set the bottle in a holder on the food tray and gaze up at him. If the electricity between them could be seen, it would resemble flashes of lightning in a thunder-filled sky. The hum of the engines and forward motion moved him to click in her seatbelt.

"I love that you did all of this for me, but how much does something like this cost? Didn't we have a conversation about the importance of saving and investing?"

Dallas stretched his long legs and crossed them at the ankles. "This is an investment. Can you imagine me crammed into a commercial flight?"

Alicia could imagine a lot of things right now. Her gaze traveled from those long, powerful legs and thighs to his groin, which couldn't hide under the grey sweatpants. His sculpted chest and broad shoulders were perfection. But his handsome face with those gorgeous lips and thick lashes was proof that God liked to show off.

"Feel free to move about. The skies are clear, and we should have a smooth flight to Ontario," one of the brothers announced over the speaker.

Outside, the runway had faded away, and they were above the clouds. Dallas undid his seatbelt and turned to Alicia. "You didn't answer my earlier question."

They both headed to the bar.

"What question was that again? Something about a Club?" She busied herself fixing a small plate.

Dallas' arms snaked around her waist. He nuzzled her neck and kissed that sensitive spot-the groove where the neck and shoulder blade meet.

A moan escaped her lips, and the food was all but forgotten, as he spun her to face the heat full on. Dallas pulled her tighter, and Alicia stretched up on her toes to throw her arms around and trace the tight curls at the base of his neck. The kiss they shared left her breathless and him in need of obvious relief. No matter how many times they were intimate, their chemistry always felt unreal.

"Come here, baby." Dallas took her hand and guided her toward the seat. He sat and pulled Alicia to straddle him.

His growing erection felt her core through lace panties, and his lips sucked the curve of her neck. He looked into those green eyes and smiled.

"When you said we were flying to Canada, I didn't know you meant like this." Alicia ran her hands over his chest.

Dallas caressed her face with both hands. "Thank you for trusting me."

When Dallas shared the ambush he encountered during the interview, he knew her first reaction was to pack her bags. Their whirlwind romance had been fun, but she was too classy for dealing with random women, paternity tests, and public scandals. Dallas had shown her nothing but kindness, generosity, and respect. He was the type of man that lived by a moral code. He valued hard work and honesty. He was not the type of man to treat a woman as disposable.

"Good thing you're cute, or I would be out of here," Alicia teased. "I mean, how many women do you pick up at charity events?"

Dallas gathered the hem of the maxi dress she wore and worked it over her head. "I got lucky with the first one."

Dallas pushed the bra straps to the side and took a nipple in his mouth trapping the sassy retort Alicia wanted to say. He heightened her sensation by licking circles around the sensitive area while he stroked the other breast.

He captured her mouth. The intensity of their kiss deepened, and Alicia tugged at his shirt. Skin to skin is what she needed, and that wasn't close enough.

"When you promised to take me places, I never imagined this," Alicia trailed a kiss down the side of his face and sucked his earlobe.

Dallas' hands moved with urgency. He palmed her ass, squeezing her body as he connected with her.

"You like that?" he whispered while grabbing a handful of hair and pulling her head back. Her exposed neck was met with a sweep of his tongue. Dallas caressed her back, following the line of her spine to the lace of her panties.

A reply hovered between them. Anticipation and need were almost unbearable. Her body was humming with desire.

And then a coolness came between them. Dallas kissed her nose and adjusted himself as her eyes jerked open at the sudden interruption to their connection. Sweatpants were discarded along with her moist panties. He pushed a button on the seat, and it reclined.

Dallas laid back and stared at her. He stroked his erection and licked his lips. Then he extended the other hand, and she didn't hesitate to climb back on his lap.

"I'm all yours," he said.

He watched with hooded eyes as Alicia eased down on him and an electric current flowed through her. Dallas held her still for a second and then began moving slowly. The sensual rhythm of their bodies hummed as they moaned.

Dallas gripped her thighs before settling on her hips. She watched as his body tightened and the facial expressions he made from the pleasure she gave him. He pulled her deeper, causing her to take the full length of him and claimed him completely. Dallas put his temple to Alicia's as she rocked back and forth. Her mouth found his again, and they exchanged breathy whispers and moans. Her breasts bounced between his lips, and he feasted on them until her nipples were rock hard.

The pace quickened.

Dallas thrust into Alicia as she rolled her hips and slammed back. They matched each other stroke for stroke. The only sound filtering through was the hum of the plane and her cries of "Dallas…."

He clamped onto her, and then they were heart to heart as the climax suspended them in time. Dallas pulled her close and kept moving, stroking her until the last shudder left her body, and she was spent.

"I love you, Alicia," Dallas whispered. He lifted her chin and pressed a kiss to her lips. "I love you, and I don't want you to leave. Will you stay with me a little longer?"

Alicia nodded in agreement. She would stay.

Dallas held on to that promise although his heart ached to hear three other words spill from her lips. Was she falling in love with him too?

Chapter 5

Dallas watched as Alicia stirred in the king-size bed. The white down comforter was pulled slightly under her chin, with one of her creamy thighs peeking out the side. He walked to the corner of the bed and kneeled before he placed soft kisses on the exposed skin. The moan that escaped Alicia went straight to his groin.

"Hmmm," came again from her. He licked straight up to her leg but refrained from exploring further although her intimate fragrance beckoned him to taste her there.

"Wake up, sleepy head, we have to get going. I have a lot planned for us today," Dallas whispered in her ear as he kissed the smooth curve of her neck.

He watched as Alicia's eyes fluttered open, before lowering to stare at him. "Why do we have to go so early? I thought this was a vacation."

They had arrived at their hotel late last night. After cleaning up they crashed between the luxurious sheets on the king-size bed.

"I have something important I want you to experience." He lifted the covers and laid beside her on the bed.

Dallas wanted to learn some of Canada's special history and share the moments with Alicia.

"But it's cold outside right now. At least wait two hours for it to warm up a few degrees." Alicia whined.

He put his arms around her, pulling her closer to his chest. "You have thirty minutes to shower and dress, or I'll be forced to wash you myself."

"This must really be important, if you're giving up two hours in bed with me." She glanced back at him before freeing herself and heading to the bathroom.

Dallas stood, adjusted himself and laced his Timberland boots. "It's very important for me to share this amazing time with my beautiful lady."

"Challenge accepted." Alicia replied from the threshold. "Thirty minutes or less."

He took a seat on the sofa and turned the television to the sports channel before he responded, "I have to see this. I have never known a woman that could be ready in that short of a time."

Alicia threw a small bottle of lotion at him, which Dallas caught in one hand. She pushed the door closed and locked it just as he ran toward her.

"I know what you're doing. Stop stalling." He returned to his seat only to see a repeat of the interview he'd had before leaving Texas. The news had gotten picked up from the local station and was now a national trending topic. He immediately placed a call to his agent.

"Katie, I thought you had a handle on that situation from the interview. I can't even enjoy my vacation without seeing that playing on TV."

"Good morning to you too, Dallas," she responded in a dry tone.

"Sorry, Good Morning, but I need to know who this person is and why they would make up this lie about me." He glanced at the bathroom door. He didn't want to keep rehashing this with Alicia.

Dallas listened to Katie shout orders at someone through her phone.

This was why she was his agent. Tough, thorough, and tenacious, with a bark that was a warning for her bite.

"I apologize for that. Trust that I am working on the situation, and it'll be resolved before you get back to the States. First, I'm trying to squash all the media hype behind this. By the way, Kim is in hot water. The network is threatening to fire her."

Dallas listened to the shower still running. "She should be fired. Who reports a story that hasn't been vetted? Kim has pushed the boundaries of professionalism for a while but coming at me like that, she's got it twisted."

"I got you covered. Haven't I always had your back?" Katie's voice was muffled as the connection cut in and out. "Don't answer that. Enjoy yourself. Later."

She disconnected the call. Dallas put his head down and tried hard to wrap his mind around this. There was nothing he could do about it here, so he had to put it out of his mind for the time. When he looked up, Alicia was standing in the door, smiling at him.

"How's that for timing?" Alicia struck a pose and threw her fur lined parka over one shoulder.

With a quick glance at his watch, he responded, "Not bad. One minute to spare, I can't believe it." He sauntered over to where she stood and placed a kiss on her forehead. "You are gorgeous."

"Thank you. You're not too shabby yourself," she responded with a playful wink. "Let's get out of here before I think of other things to do with you."

Dallas rushed her to the waiting car he had reserved to drive them to their first destination. A quick breakfast was in order at Falls Side Restaurant.

"I heard they have excellent breakfast here. Let's fuel up because we have a long day ahead of us." He helped her out of the car after they reached the café.

The restaurant from all appearances was a popular place. So, many familiar smells permeated the air as they made their entrance. Bacon, pancakes, cinnamon, and pastries.

"Just two?" The bubbly, red-haired waitress asked while grabbing two menus, but not waiting for on a response. "Follow me, please."

She led them to a table overlooking Niagara Falls. The view was breathtaking even from the restaurant's window, but the look of amazement on Alicia's face was priceless.

"Dallas, this is beautiful." She stared out of the window for a few minutes, before she grabbed his hand. "Thank you, for this. I kept trying to figure out why you would bring me somewhere so cold when tropical and warm would be so much better."

He gripped her hand tighter. "We've done the beaches in Jamaica already. I remember you mentioning that this was on your list of places to come. With the commercial shoot and community events, I thought this was the perfect time to explore. Let's order some food, and then we can get started." Dallas signaled for the waitress who was delivering drinks at the table in front of theirs.

"Are you ready to order?" The freckle-faced lady asked. She had to be a teenager or early twenties, because there was not a wrinkle to be seen.

Dallas ordered true to the basketball player that he is-- enough food for two people. Alicia went the simpler route, spinach and feta omelet, toast with peach butter, coffee, and water.

"I'll be right back with your drinks once I place your order." She took their menus and headed towards the kitchen.

"Are you going to tell me what's going on?" Alicia asked. Even though she loved the mystery of him trying to surprise her, that typically didn't turn out in her favor. Maybe it was just that the surprises her family provided were ones where she ended up on the giving end.

"I will give you one clue a day, only to keep you curious. This way I ensure you give me a little more time. How does that sound?" Dallas asked just as the waitress returned with their drinks. She placed their drinks and informed them their food would be up next and moved on to the next table.

"That doesn't sound like a win to me. Besides, I'm beginning to think trouble is following us, since everywhere we've been something strange occurs." She grumbled and fiddled with her silverware. "I don't do drama."

"It'll be worth it. I promise." Dallas took a drink of apple juice and looked around. People were scattered throughout the space engaged in their own conversations and enjoying their meals. He loved traveling abroad and the sense of privacy it provided. He bet no one here even recognized him which was preferable with the false story circulating the news.

"Oh, you're worth it. But promises don't mean anything. I'm more of a show me type of lady," Alicia replied. They carried on with their conversation for another fifteen minutes until their food arrived.

As the plates were placed on the table, Dallas' stomach rumbled so loud that people from the next table laughed. "Sorry, but this smells so good, and I'm starving." He and Alicia joined in the laughter before blessing their food and diving in.

She watched Dallas stuff a bite of pancakes and sausage in his mouth, "This is pretty good."

Alicia spread some peach butter on her toast and took a sip of her coffee. After seasoning her omelet to her taste, she took a bite of the toast. "Hmm this peach butter is divine. I may have to steal a biscuit and try it there as well."

The waitress came around topping off their beverages as the waitstaff cleaned tables nearby and prepared for the next guests.

"You can have anything on my plate your heart desires." He picked up a biscuit and spread the peach butter for her and placed it on her plate. Dallas licked his lips before saying, "Would you like anything else?" He followed that with a slow roll of his tongue across his bottom lip.

Alicia shifted in her seat and took a bite of the biscuit. A dollop of peach butter was on the corner of her mouth, and Dallas leaned over and kissed it off, sat back in his seat and continued his meal as though nothing out of the ordinary had happened.

She responded to his earlier question, "I think you've done enough Mister, stay in your seat."

Both laughed after her comment and finished their meals. He typed something into his phone while he waited for the waitress to return with the bill. "You ready for the next adventure?"

Alicia rubbed her stomach. "More like ready for a nap, but what do you have up your sleeve?"

Dallas looked up his sleeve, "Just my arm," and doubled over in laughter at his lame joke. He paid the bill and pulled out her chair. "Let's get out of here."

"Always the jokester." She walked out in front of him to the car where the driver waited with the door held open. They slid right inside to the warm car seats.

They arrived at their next stop, Niagara Helicopter Tours. Dallas exited the car and spoke with the pilots, while the driver assisted Alicia. After a brief conversation, he returned and took her hand, "Ready?"

She halted her steps. "Where are we going?"

"I'm not telling." Dallas grinned and tried to pull her along.

Alicia stood firm. "You are if you want me to get in that thing."

"The Falls." He gestured to the landscape surrounding them. "We're going to see the Falls."

"I thought we would see them with our feet planted firmly on the ground."

Dallas pulled her in his arms. "But this will give you an aerial view. You'll like it so much better. Trust me."

They walked close to the chopper. Dallas coaxed her by whispering how much he loved her in her ear. He helped her in the bird before climbing in himself. Once they were both strapped in, the guides gave a few instructions, and they were in the air.

Alicia relaxed once they took off but still had a tight grip on his hand. The proximity of the helipad to the falls was minimal. Before she could prepare herself for the scenic view, the beauty and majesty of the waterfall stole her breath.

"Dallas, from below you get the feel of the water and the sense of danger from the force of the falls. But nothing compares to seeing three bodies of water intertwined into one of the most hypnotic sites I've ever seen in my life. Thank you for this experience." She kissed him and was silent for the remainder of the twelve-minute flight. He practically missed the scenery because he was watching the force of nature sitting beside him. The sense of wonder on her face outshone the beauty of the Falls.

Once they landed, the tour guide helped her down from the helicopter. "Ready for your next adventure?"

"I doubt if anything will top what I just experienced."

After they were seated in the car, Dallas turned to face her, "Promise me a few more days."

Alicia was enjoying her time with him, but she had qualms about what was happening in their relationship. She would give him a little time but could not guarantee him forever.

Alicia touched Dallas' cheek. "I think that can be arranged Mr. Avery."

Chapter 6

"Noah Ang Haun. Why are you hanging out here so much?"

He froze in place as he came face to face with his mother, Noelle. Based on the frown and use of his entire name, Noah knew he was in trouble.

"Hey, Mom." Noah cleared his throat and flashed a smile. "How's your day going?"

Noelle would not be charmed by her son. "Don't hey me. What are you doing here?"

The here she was referring to was Noah's usual shortcut out of the hotel which took him down the concrete corridor past the hotel laundry room. He wasn't expecting his mother to emerge around the corner.

"Looking for you," Noah said. He didn't tell her he was coming from delivering food to Jada's room. Fortunately, what Jada thought were labor pains yesterday went away, and she'd been resting ever since. Noah had someone on standby for when the delivery day came.

Noelle clucked her disbelief and pushed through the double doors leading to the washroom. Noah followed.

Industrial-sized washers churned with bed linens and dryers hummed with towels. Two large fans in each corner of the room couldn't compete with the heat.

"Looking for me, huh?" Noelle positioned herself behind a large table stacked with a jumble of freshly laundered items. "Shouldn't you still be in school?"

Noah spoke to a passing worker. At least three other housekeeping staff buzzed around preparing the carts with items to clean the rooms.

"It's a half-day," Noah lied. He hadn't been in school for a couple of days. He knew Jada's dad would probably look for him there. He heard Tony was on a rampage when he discovered Jada was gone. Noah was interrogated for an hour, but he stuck to his story about Jada sneaking out without him knowing anything. So far, his deception was good enough to buy them some time.

Noelle folded the pristine white sheet in her hand and pulled another from the basket. "School is your top priority. Education is important and your ticket to a better life."

"I know, Mom." He'd heard her education speech many times before so pretended to listen while he watched her. Sweat glistened on her forehead. A few strands of jet-black hair clung to her face where they had escaped the bun she wore as part of the drab gray housekeeping uniform. The clunky black shoes supported swollen ankles. Noah knew education was important, but his main concern was helping pay bills. Working for the cartel was more lucrative than sitting in Algebra class.

"Mr. Tony came by the apartment last night."

Noah's heart drummed loud enough to drown out the buzzing signaling a load was complete.

"What did he want?" Noah swallowed his dread and hoped his mom didn't notice.

She wiped sweat from her brow. "He said you got his daughter in trouble, and she's gone missing. Do you know anything about that?"

The question hung between them, and Noah's mind raced. He didn't want to lie to his mother anymore, but he would do anything to protect her.

"Mom, I…", he began, but Noelle tossed a towel on the table and silenced him with a look.

"Follow me."

Noah followed her down the hall to the freight elevator. She didn't speak again until the doors closed.

"Too many ears in there," she said and punched the button for the lobby.

"I don't want you working for that gang," she continued. "You think you're helping me, but I'll work three jobs to make sure we're okay. Tony took your father away from me. You're all I have left. I can't lose you too."

Noah looked into his mother's eyes. The pain of losing his dad was evident in her wide eyes. He was killed two years ago under murky circumstances. All they knew was he did a job for Tony. How long he was a part of the cartel remained a mystery, but Mom believed he was trying to get out. And no one walked away from Tony.

"You don't have to worry about me." Noah pulled her into an embrace. She was only tall enough to reach his chin.

"I'm your mother." Noelle brushed bangs from Noah's face. "I'll always worry about my baby. But I know you'll do the right thing. I told Tony you would handle your responsibilities for the baby. Although I'm too young to be a grandmother."

The elevator doors chimed and opened on the lobby floor. His mother hurried down the hall, and he ran to catch up.

"Wait, what? Grandmother? You think…" Noah's words lodged in his throat when he saw Dallas Avery at the front desk.

Noelle turned to her son. "Isn't that the ball player you're always talking about? You should go say 'hi'."

He shook his head. "No. I mean, yeah, it's him, but I don't want to bother the man. Talk to you later, Mom."

Noah raced out the door after assuring his mother he would go straight home. And he would.

But first, he had to tell Jada their way out had checked into the hotel.

Chapter 6

"What is this I hear about you getting some young woman pregnant, and you refuse to take her call?" Anna Avery roared on the other end of the line. "Dallas Avery, what did I tell you before you made it to high school? If you don't wrap it, you can't tap it."

Dallas closed his eyes. "Mom, if you would let me get a word in for just a second, you'd know it's just a rumor." Dallas pulled the phone away from his ear long enough to tap for the driver to raise the privacy screen. Their car ride had been filled with flirtatious banter until this call.

"Do I need to call Katie and get her to manage this for you, since you're on vacation and all," she snapped.

Dallas mouthed to Alicia, "I'm so sorry," while simultaneously shaking his head.

"Let me ask you; are you protecting yourself with *this* one?"

He was glad that Alicia was already aware of the situation because the last thing he needed was to have explain. He was already banking against hope that their relationship wasn't doomed. How much could he ask this woman to take?

"I'm not discussing that with you, Mama. It's not like I'm still sixteen. Trust I've got this covered, and we can discuss it when I get back stateside. Now, please just take care of you. I'm handling this."

She groaned, and he pictured her stomping a foot on the kitchen tile. "Alright Son, I'll let you slide this time because you're with your lady friend. But don't ever think you're too grown that I won't go upside your head, Mister. I love you."

"No ma'am, not at all. I love you." Dallas crossed his heart saying a prayer that his mother didn't disown him when he returned, but he didn't want to have this discussion right now.

Dallas wanted children, and if the tables were turned and the rumors were concerning Alicia, he would be ecstatic. He just needed more time with her for her to see he really was a stand-up guy.

"I apologize for that…" His apology was thwarted by the hand she was holding up.

"Dallas, I don't need an apology. You've already explained. If I were your mother, I'd want to make sure you were fine and trying to find this woman." She lowered her hand and relinked it with his. "Let's enjoy the rest of our trip."

"Did I tell you I started the stock portfolio we discussed on our first date?" Dallas pulled his phone from his coat, typed into an app, and handed the phone over. "And I'm doing well. At least I believe so."

She plucked the phone from his and scrolled through the app. "I'd say you're doing great."

"My broker says I should make one million in less than two years." He winked.

She glanced out the window, then toward the privacy screen the driver had raised earlier. Alicia didn't give her investment strategy to just anyone. "I won't steer you wrong."

"Thank you. You're the best. In more ways than one." He checked his phone when it beeped. "We'll be at the airport in five minutes. Then our destination in seventeen. After this stop, food and we can get some rest. How does that sound?"

Since they were boarding a private plane, they avoided all gates and other terminals on the way to the hanger. "Yes, rest would be nice," she responded.

Dallas helped her out of the car and onto the plane.

After Alicia was seated and resting, Dallas stepped away to speak with the pilot.

"Dallas," she called when she reached for his hand but came up empty. He wasn't in the main cabin

"You called?" Dallas asked as he slid into the seat opposite her, picked up her foot and massaged it working his way up her leg.

"I wanted to thank you for that trip to the Falls. It was spectacular."

He picked up the other leg and placed it on his lap. "Couldn't just bring you over here to keep you in bed, because you deserve more than that."

"Dallas, I…" she whispered.

"Save all of that until we get back home," he warned. "This is a vacation for both of us; serious stuff can wait." A ping of his phone notified him that they were landing. "Buckle up, we're here."

She touched his hand but said nothing else as she buckled her seatbelt.

Once deplaned and in the vehicle, she asked, "What are we doing now?"

"Do you remember the story of Uncle Tom's Cabin?"

She paused, filtering through her memories. "Yes, I know the tale. But what does that have to do with Canada? His story was set in the United States."

The car came to a stop, and Dallas smiled at her. "Hold that thought, and you will see." He exited the vehicle and helped her out of the car. "This is the real cabin that belonged to Josiah Henson."

Alicia scanned the massive property they stood on. A tour guide dressed in khaki pants with a matching jacket awaited their arrival at the entrance of the cabin. The baseball cap was unable to tame the shock of red hair. She couldn't wait to find out more about this place.

"Come let's go in." Dallas took her hand leading the way.

"Welcome, my name is Francois, and I'll be your guide for today. Please follow me this way." He extended his muscular arm to lead them through the adjacent gift shop displaying an assortment of souvenirs. Then they walked past a conference room where Francois mentioned the monthly lecture series featuring past speakers of academic acclaim. They left that space and went into a side room full of colorful banners and transparent glass displays.

Alicia was disturbed by the exhibit showing the whips and chains and quickly moved away. Francois explained, "Ma'am, while that is a painful part of history, it's also a relevant one. We have to embrace the painful past to move to a productive future. Our displays are not to glorify slavery, but to show the inhuman treatment of human beings."

"Sometimes, it's tough to see and realize our ancestors suffered through so much just so we could be free."

Alicia laced her arm through Dallas', praying it would give her strength to make it through this exhibit.

Francois clarified "Josiah was a slave in Maryland, who was trying to buy his freedom. But he was hoodwinked by his owner to be sold in New Orleans. He took his family and fled to Canada. I'm sure this proved even more difficult since he was maimed by a beating from a previous owner."

Dallas gave Alicia's shoulder a gentle squeeze. "How is his story related to the one in the United States?"

Francois directed them to another display. "It is believed that Josiah and Ms. Beecher-Stowe were acquainted and that her story is indeed based on his real life. After settling in Canada, he became a major conductor and was key in helping other slaves escape through the Underground Railroad. Several times he took the passage in reverse to help others escape. Mr. Henson preached, but he also convinced his friends to put their money in with him to purchase this property. Two hundred acres of land, so that other fugitive slaves would have a safe place to start over. There was a school, church, several houses and once we walk outside, I will show you something pretty special."

They walked through the remainder of the indoor tour checking out each exhibit and listening to Francois. He gave them a tour of the house and church and showed them a sycamore tree where the trunk had been turned into a smokehouse to cure meat.

"Thank you, Francois, for being such a great tour guide," Alicia and Dallas both agreed on that point.

"You are most welcome." He shook their hands and thanked them for coming. He handed a card and pamphlet to Dallas with more information on contacts for history on the slave trade.

"I have a few more places to show you," Dallas confessed. "But that will be tomorrow."

Chapter 8

Alicia swiped to end the call and tossed her cell phone on the bed. She ran both hands through her shoulder-length hair in an attempt to contain the mounting frustration.

"Is everything okay?" Dallas closed the door and placed the bag of food on the nearby table. He crossed the room in two strides and gathered her in his arms.

The beat of his heart against her was the balm she didn't know she needed. "Family drama," she said into his chest. "No matter where I go, their problems seem to follow."

"Want to talk about it? I don't want to pry."

Alicia had only revealed the basic stats about her family. He knew both her parents were deceased. The tragic backstory was shared when a thunderstorm triggered a memory about the night her mother and father were killed in a car accident. Her grandmother along with Alicia's twin were killed by the twister that ripped through their house. She told him a few stories about growing up with her brother and the gambling addict he turned into. Dallas knew she despised her sister-in-law but doted on her niece.

Alicia shook her head and stepped back. "Same old story. My brother messes up; his scheming wife prompts my niece to call me, and everyone expects me to write a check to clean it up."

"Survivor's guilt can be stressful." Dallas sat on the bed but reached out for Alicia's hand. "My sister and her trifling husband do me the same way. It's hard to tell family 'No' when they know you can afford it."

"The best thing I did was leave them in Chicago. I even let them live in my house, just to have peace of mind, but it's never enough." Alicia thought back to all the times she had bailed James and Bernice out of dire situations. They seemed to think her dead husband left her a pot of gold. He did leave her comfortable, but it was her own hard work and stock savvy which turned her inheritance into enough money to travel the world. She considered it back pay for the years she endured a loveless marriage from a grown man who pounced the moment she turned sixteen.

Dallas tugged and settled Alicia on his lap. He stroked her face and placed a kiss on her nose. "Can't really blame them though. I can't get enough of you either."

Alicia poked him in the ribs and laughed. "You are a mess, Mr. Avery. Did I thank you for helping me check this adventure off my list?"

His gaze turned serious. "I believe you did, but I'm open for more acts of gratitude." Dallas trailed a hand down her face and massaged a nipple through her sweater.

Alicia squirmed as the first trickles of pleasure stirred. She couldn't believe how in sync their bodies always were. Her lips sought his like a magnet, and their tongues began their own intimate dance. "I can't get enough of you either," she whispered.

The dinner was forgotten as they feasted on each other. All thoughts of family and outside drama were replaced with the physical need to nurture each other.

Clothes were shed. Alicia laid back as Dallas kissed her neck and took his acrobatic tongue on a journey to explore her most intimate parts. She leaned up and watched the top of his head bob between her legs. This was a man worth surrendering to. Dallas was the most generous man in every way. He deserved the world.

"Dallas, oh, Dallas," she cried. Her body clenched as the orgasm suspended her body, and shockwaves of pleasure took over.

When she regained consciousness, Dallas stared at her with a satisfied smirk. He licked his lips. "Good to the last drop."

Alicia tried to kick a leg, but the aftershock of his skillful oral game delayed feeling from returning. "You think you're all of that, don't 'cha?"

He climbed in bed to lie beside her. "Nope. I just know I want you to feel good. Now say you'll stay with me another day."

"You know at some point we'll have to get back to the real world." She ran a hand down his chiseled chest and claimed the erection that throbbed between them.

Dallas could barely speak. "Woman, the things you do to me."

Alicia continued to stroke him and watched as he closed his eyes and moaned. His facial expressions showed his desire. She loved it. She loved this man. But could she really give him all he wanted and deserved?

Dallas stilled her hand and lifted her chin. "Say you'll stay."

The man was persistent.

Alicia nodded and ceased further discussion by taking him in her mouth. Nothing else needed to be said.

Chapter 9

"Wake up baby," Dallas whispered in Alicia's ear before moving down to uncover her foot.

"Heeeeyyy." It took all of three seconds for Alicia to kick him clean off the bed.

"What was that for," he asked as he slowly got up from the floor.

"You tickled my feet! Who does that?" She stretched out in the bed, arms above her head. "I was sleeping good, and I hate being tickled."

Dallas had ordered room service for them, since they never got around to eating the dinner he picked up. He'd allowed Alicia to sleep in this morning because he wanted to keep her out just a little later tonight and tomorrow before they headed back to the States.

After the workout they had last night, he was famished and was pretty sure that she was too. Which didn't require much guessing on his part since her stomach was growling earlier, but not enough to wake her from her slumber. He was the only one he knew that would wake up when his stomach growled, but that usually meant he'd slept too long.

"My apologies pretty lady, but breakfast is here, and I didn't want it to get cold." Dallas went over to the dining area of the suite. Room service had delivered two place settings with steaming trays of food. "Come over, and I'll fix you a plate.

Alicia sauntered over to the bar and fixed coffee for her and Dallas, while he prepared their plates.

"The commercial shoot has been postponed so all I need to do today is make an appearance at the Community Center. After that, we'll do some shopping."

"First dibs on the shower," Alicia blurted out as she ran to the bathroom.

Dallas followed close behind but didn't catch her. "That was not fair."

"All's fair in love and hot water." Alicia laughed and closed the door.

Dallas cleaned up their breakfast dishes and put the trash in the chute outside their room. Once he stepped back inside, Alicia was sitting in bed wrapped in a thick, white cotton bath sheet applying lotion to her legs. "Woman, you are so sexy." He crossed the room in what seemed like two long steps.

She put up a greased hand. "Mr., go shower so we can get out of here before we miss all the great shopping."

"Oh, I see. You rushed to dress because I said the magic word."

Alicia's laughter filled the room. "Of course, I'm a woman, and we love to shop. So please hurry."

Dallas kissed her cheek. "I'm going." He grabbed the shaving kit and headed to the shower.

When he walked out fifteen minutes later, he found Alicia bent over tying her shoes, and what a sight she was to behold. He sneaked up behind up and held her. She didn't budge when he wrapped his arm around her waist; she only leaned her head back to his shoulder and kissed his neck. He released her and finished dressing.

"Let's do this. See if we can break the bank." He winked and waited for her at the door.

The Spalding Community Center was a whirlwind of activity. The sound of bouncing balls and squeaking sneakers on the hardwood had

Dallas in his element. A representative from NBA Cares, the NBA's social program, had scheduled an impromptu skill showcase and then Dallas passed out backpacks and posed for pictures. Alicia sat on some bleachers and watched him engage with the children.

After an hour of that, they went to Twenty Valley. Alicia was in heaven. One hundred and ten glorious shops for her to stroll through. She picked up a purple raincoat and matching umbrella from Arezzo, adding to her collection of rain gear purchased from everywhere she traveled.

They shopped for three hours, and Dallas swore someone was following them. "Let's get a sandwich here," he pointed at the Grand Oak Culinary Market. "I want to make sure this kid isn't following us."

"How do you plan to do that without being seen?" Alicia asked.

Dallas lowered his voice. "We're going to go in and place an order." He opened the door. "Then we will sit down, and I'll go to the restroom and sneak around behind him. How does that sound?"

They walked to the counter and placed an order for club sandwiches and took a seat. Dallas turned his camera on and reversed it like he was taking a selfie. He could see a young black-haired boy peaking around the corner. He tilted it a little further and saw the black, ripped jeans and black combat boots. He smiled and took a picture so he would have one for later if he couldn't catch him.

"I'm not sure it will work, but it's worth a try," Alicia replied.

"I'll be right back." Dallas stood and pushed his chair in, gave Alicia a quick kiss on the cheek, and glanced at the door before heading toward opposite the door.

By the time he made it around to the front, the young man was nowhere to be seen. Dallas only took four steps to reach Alicia. "Where did he go?"

"He waited a few minutes and walked away," she said as she picked up her sandwich, taking a bite.

"Maybe he didn't get an autograph at the community center." Dallas shrugged and joined Alicia in polishing off the meal. Maybe he was just paranoid with the potential scandal brewing for him back home. He made a mental note to check in with Katie when they returned to the room.

"We don't have to shop any more. Let's finish eating and just return to the room," Alicia suggested.

"That's fine," Dallas responded as he cleared the table.

Hand in hand they left the restaurant, and Dallas ran straight into the young guy and knocked him down.

"Why are you following us?" Dallas asked but received no response as the youngster hurried to his feet and took off around the corner of the building.

Before he turned to run after him, Dallas felt Alicia stiffen, causing him to stop dead in his tracks at the expression on her face.

"Dallas," was the only word that escaped.

Chapter 10

"Keep her safe."

Alicia had released Dallas' hand to get a grip on the baby that was thrust into her arms. The girl, a baby herself, blinked back tears and wiped sweat from her brow with trembling fingers. "Keep her safe," she repeated and tore off down the sidewalk in the same direction as the young man.

Dallas peered at the squirming bundle Alicia cradled against her bosom. "What's going on? Is that a baby?"

One minute they were laughing and shopping. The next minute they were being followed and suddenly what: parents, or at least caretakers for a stranger's child.

People passed by on the sidewalk, and a few seemed to have witnessed the strange transaction. Curious glances caused Alicia to move toward their waiting vehicle.

The baby made cooing sounds as she rooted around Alicia's chest. Slick, black hair was matted to the tiny head, and her body was covered in a thin coat of mucus and blood. Someone had taken care to clean the little, round face.

"This is a newborn." Alicia rocked the infant. "Did that child just give us her baby?"

The baby nestled in Alicia's arm let out a small yawn and snuggled in closer. She caressed the fragile head and twirled a finger around a wayward strand of silky, straight black hair.

"Why would someone try to give you away?" she whispered.

Alicia knew all too well that some babies were seen as inconvenient and were thrown to whomever would catch them. Her mind replayed the last time it happened to her. Although, that child was related to her through blood. Bernice, her brother's trifling wife, had signed into the hospital as Alicia and had a baby in secret, setting up Alicia to take care of her. Something she helpfully did for five years, despite the objections from Patrick, her deceased husband. It broke her heart when James learned the truth and demanded that Bernice get his daughter back. Not that she could blame him.

But that was the past. This baby was not her niece. Remembering the angelic face of her niece was in total reflection of this sleeping bundle in her arms. Alicia tucked the blanket around an alabaster fist with a blush of sand which was proof of the child's mixed heritage. Probably Asian and Black.

"Should we try to find Mr. Avery?" Liam, the chauffeur, asked interrupting her examination of the infant.

She'd almost forgotten the white-haired driver was in the vehicle. Dallas joked that he looked like the actor Richard Gere, but this was no Pretty Woman moment.

"No, he asked us to wait. I'm sure he'll be right back," she said and shifted position on the plush leather seat.

Alicia could see the side of Liam's face in the rearview mirror. His thin lips twisted in disgust. "These runaways are nothing but trouble.

You should take that infant to the peace officers. No telling what it's been exposed to."

"We need to make sure the girl gets help. She must be desperate to give her baby to a stranger, don't you think?" Alicia had only seen the girl for a second, but she recognized the precarious nature emitting from the teenager like a siren. She had once been in that dark and lonely place.

Liam wasn't convinced. "I know how these runaways work. They pretend they're in trouble to lure you into a trap. Next thing you know, you're being robbed by their crew."

Alicia knew Dallas could handle himself. She'd seen him in action during their previous trips to Scotland and Jamaica. Those adventures only drew them closer.

"Well, I know scared, and that girl was scared. Dallas will bring her back, and we'll sort out this whole thing."

"Americans," Liam mumbled with a shake of his head.

Alicia ignored the slight. His comments did make her question the situation though. She hoped it was simply a girl with no one to help. But what if Liam was right, and Dallas was being hurt right now? She reached for the door handle when a flash of white appeared down the street.

Chapter 11

Dallas searched the crowded sidewalk. The restaurant was in a popular tourist area heavily populated with various restaurants and shops. He spotted the girl standing at the corner where the young man had disappeared, partially hidden by a metal recycling receptacle.

"I'm going to see if she's alright," he told Alicia. Dodging an old couple pushing a cart of groceries, Dallas was able to cover the distance before the girl had time to react. Her eyes widened at this approach, and she turned to rush down the alley. She had a head start, but Dallas' long athletic stride and the fact that she just delivered a baby, meant he easily caught her.

"Hold on," Dallas grabbed the girl's arm but released it when she jerked away. "Sorry. I'm sorry, but please stop."

The girl looked up at him and backed away. Her small hands were in fists as though she was prepared to fight.

Dallas knew he was dealing with a frightened child and relaxed his shoulders. Showing his palms, he stayed still and didn't try to touch her again. "Are you alright?"

The girl didn't answer.

"Are you hurt?" He could see the girl needed medical attention. The growing blood stain on her pants indicated that. He took one small step toward her.

The girl took a step back, and her eyes darted back and forth. "Are you really an American basketball player?"

Dallas removed his sunglasses. "I am. You like basketball?" He hoped some common interest would allow the girl to trust him. Although, the oversize navy hockey team jersey would denote an affinity for the national champions. The white leggings were concerning as the dark stain seemed to be growing. He needed to get this girl to come with him and Alicia.

She shook her head. "Noah does."

"Who's Noah?"

A short beep echoed from the other end of the alley. The same teenage boy dressed in ripped jeans, black t-shirt, and black combat boots sat on a motor bike. The girl gave a wave and started toward him. Dallas assumed this boy was Noah and was involved in this situation. *Is he the baby's father?*

"Hey, wait," Dallas called to the girl's retreating back. "What's your name?"

The girl continued moving without answering. Something or someone out of Dallas' sight caused Noah to turn and almost fall off the bike. He righted himself and pointed back toward Dallas. "Jada, run!"

Noah revved the bike and took off in the opposite direction, leaving a trail of smoke behind.

The girl, Jada, froze for a second and then hobbled toward Dallas. She almost made it past him before he could react.

"They're coming." Jada motioned for Dallas to move.

He didn't know what they were running from, but Dallas knew whatever was chasing her, would soon be chasing them. He scooped her up in his arms and ran like he was on a fast break and about to make the dunk of his life. Running down the street, dodging bodies, and trying to reach the car, he screamed "Open the door".

The driver sprinted to comply and ran back to the steering wheel. Dallas slid Jada in the car and eased in behind her just as a black town car pulled up beside them.

"Drive," Dallas yelled.

Chapter 12

"Go, man. Go," Dallas commanded as he and Jada scrambled into the car.

The door barely closed before Liam pressed the gas and sent the vehicle lurking forward. "Where to, sir?"

"Dallas, what's going on?" Alicia looked between him and the girl. "Are you both okay? Is somebody chasing you?" She mimed buckling up, and Jada snapped her seatbelt into place.

He raised a hand to pause Alicia's question and turned to the driver. "Take us back to the hotel, please." Then he pressed the button to raise the partition dividing the front seat.

Alicia raised her eyebrows, and he nodded at her silent question. They needed privacy for this conversation.

"This is Jada." Dallas introduced their guest to Alicia and wiped at a bead of sweat forming on his brow. His heart rate was still elevated, and he took deep breaths to get it under control. He could run up and down a basketball court for three hours, and it didn't have this effect. Of course, on the court he was trying to score a basket or prevent his opponent from scoring one. There wasn't the element of real fear. And he didn't even know what, or who, they were running from.

Alicia told Jada her name. "Would you like to hold her?"

Jada's eyes were glued on the baby since she was placed on the seat across from Alicia, but she shook her head. Then she sat on her hands as if to keep them from reaching for the child.

Dallas stretched his long legs and placed them on each side of Alicia who sat on the seat in front of him. She patted his knee, and the simple touch relaxed him.

He turned to Jada. "You need to tell us what's going on."

"She's not safe with me," Jada whispered.

"Why not?" Dallas asked.

Before she could respond, the car lurched to a stop causing them to pitch forward. Liam spoke through the glass. "Sorry, folks."

The rest of his apology was drowned out by screeching tires and the revving of a motor. The kid on the motor bike raced by their vehicle. A black SUV trailed close behind it. They all watched through the back window as the bike ran a light and made a dangerous left turn at the next block. The SUV jumped the curb trying to keep up.

Jada's eyes widened. "That's why she's not safe with me. They're trying to get her."

"Who is they?"

"The 10K Triad. They want to sell her to the highest bidder." Jada leaned forward to look out the window. The motor bike was gone, and their vehicle resumed its journey.

Alicia cradled the baby closer to her bosom. "Who wants to buy a baby?"

"That's what they do." Jada's leg bounced up and down. "Especially the girls. Sell them and no one sees them again."

Dallas looked at Alicia. He recognized the protective posture. She was ready to fight for this child. For both girls. Out of all of their adventures to date, this one would be the most heart-wrenching because there were so many dynamics they didn't know and only so much they could do.

"He said since this baby is mixed breed people pay more for them," Jada shifted in her seat. Her large brown eyes pleaded for help.

Dallas' mind searched for a solution. He knew they would help, but the vision of that boy being chased screamed danger. "What are we dealing with? Who said that? Who is he?"

The vehicle pulled into the hotel driveway

and Liam parked and left the car clearly shaken by the experience.

"Who is he?" Dallas repeated.

Jada seemed to shrink against the door. "The leader of the cartel. My father."

Chapter 13

"Here's what I found out." Dallas ended his cell phone call and crossed the room where Alicia sat on the bed. The baby was centered with a makeshift arrangement of pillows propped around her. Jada was in the shower.

He kissed the top of Alicia's head, taking in her unique scent of lavender and vanilla. Even with all the chaos around them, he longed for her. The chemistry between them was so strong, he couldn't be alone with her without wanting to touch her. To taste her. But he would settle for kneeling between those thighs. He was rewarded with Alicia's arm wrapping around his neck and pulling him close.

"Thank you." The words caressed his ears, and he pressed his head against her bosom. People say you're lucky if you find your soulmate. Dallas knew Alicia was his.

"What are you thanking me for?"

She lifted his chin, and her green eyes bore into his. "In case I don't get a chance to say it later. Thank you for being you."

"I can only be me," he joked. Although he understood she was vocalizing her appreciation for his actions.

Alicia had already arranged for baby supplies through the hotel's concierge. So as soon as they returned to the hotel, he got his Canadian trainer to send over a medical doctor to check on Jada. Surprisingly, whoever assisted in the birth did an excellent job. The blood stain Dallas saw earlier was due to the absence of a feminine pad and not a botched delivery or the placenta remaining inside. That solved one mystery, but a more pressing one remained.

Who was the 10K Triad?

Dallas needed law enforcement for that one and based on Jada's assessment, the local peace officers could not be trusted. He was able to get in touch with Alex Williams, an Atlanta detective. They became close when Alex worked security at the Atlanta Hawks game and some aggressive fans attempted to board the team bus. Alex led Dallas to a safe room until the fans were disbursed. A friendship was born in those forty minutes.

"Alex was able to get some intel from a colleague here. They worked undercover on some joint drug task force together. Name's Oliver Smith." Dallas rose from the altar although the warmth beckoned him to return. He needed to focus on their current situation and get the four of them out of the country safely.

Alicia must have felt his absence too. She wrapped her arms around herself and rubbed her hands up and down. "Can this Oliver guy be trusted? Jada said this Triad has people on the police force."

Dallas nodded. "Alex vouched for him. Says he's a 'by the book' guy. Anyway, he has extensive files on this group. Says they've been tracking them for years. They'll catch a few members, but no one talks. They're into everything. Drugs, weapons, sex trafficking. Peace officers here have had secret raids foiled. Several law enforcement men and women have been arrested for assisting this group. And it all comes back to their leader who no one can ever pin any charges on. Tony Soto. Esteemed businessman and philanthropist by day. Criminal mastermind by night."

"And my Dad."

Dallas and Alicia turned toward the bathroom. Jada had emerged, hair still damp from the shower. The hotel gift shop had provided the Canada sweatpants and shirt she now wore on her small frame.

Alicia left the bed and stood in front of Jada. "Feeling better?"

Jada nodded. "Thanks for the clothes. And everything."

"No need for that," Alicia raised her arms to hug Jada but paused. "We're going to help you, okay?"

The affirmative answer came with Jada stepping into Alicia and holding on. Sobs wrecked her body. Dallas hung back, sensing that a male presence wasn't needed. He learned from Alex that Tony Soto's wife had died last year. A suicide, and her daughter was the one to find the body. Even he could recognize that Jada needed a mother.

The baby's cries caused them to separate.

"Someone's awake." Alicia returned to the other side of the bed and picked up the infant. "Are you hungry?" she cooed.

Dallas took a bottle from the mini fridge and followed Alicia's instruction for heating up the formula. He relished the act and considered it practice for when he had his own children. Alicia would make a good mother. She had gauged the baby's needs with expert precision. He gave her the bottle after testing the temperature on his wrist.

"Would you like to feed her?" Alicia asked Jada.

She shook her head and settled on the floor, crossing her legs beneath her.

"Well, does she have a name?" Dallas tried to coax some interest in the baby from Jada. "We can't keep calling her 'Baby'."

All he got was a shrug. He looked to Alicia for any ideas to break through, but her attention was on the baby.

Dallas cut on the television and scrolled through the channels. "What do you like to watch?"

Jada didn't answer at first but piped up when he made it to the Disney Channel. An animated show played advertising the next episode of *Phineas and Ferb* reminding Dallas that this girl was too young to take care of a baby. *Who had hurt her that way?*

He took a chair near her spot on the floor. "What grade are you in?"

"Just started high school. Grade 8," Jada said.

"You like school?"

She nodded. "I didn't want to be home schooled, but Father said no one could know."

Dallas quickly calculated her father didn't want people to know his daughter was pregnant. It would probably ruin his reputation.

"We'll take care of the baby," Dallas promised. "But what do *you* want to do? Do you want to go home?"

Jada's leg began bouncing. She was quiet for a beat and then blurted, "I want Noah."

Alicia burped the baby over one shoulder and mouthed a question to Dallas. "Who's Noah?"

He walked over to her and lowered his voice. "The boy on the bike. I think he was helping her."

"The boy who was being chased. How can we find him?" Alicia placed the baby back in the makeshift crib on the bed. "Someone has a full stomach and fell asleep."

Dallas pulled out his phone. "Maybe I can get Alex's contact to put out a notice or something."

The sound of a lock disengaging caused them all to turn toward the door. A figure rushed in and slammed the door.

Jada leaped from the floor. "Noah!"

Chapter 14

"You made it." Jada hugged Noah and grinned up at him.

"How did you get in here?" Dallas crossed to the door and opened it, checking the hallway for any other intruders.

Noah twirled a plastic square between his thin fingers. "Swiped a housekeeping card. My mother works here."

Dallas bolted the door with both security locks and glared at them. "You could have knocked."

"Yeah, but I like to make an entrance," he shot back, grinning. "Did you see the way I shook off those goons trying to catch me?" Noah scanned the room, his gaze landed on the stainless-steel appliances and fully stocked bar. "This is really nice. Haven't been in the suites here before."

Alicia smoothed the baby's back. She had begun to stir from the loud noise. "You need to keep it down."

Noah smiled, as his eyes latched onto the baby girl. "My bad. Sorry, miss." He turned to Jada, giving her a quick once-over. "You, okay?"

She nodded and plopped back on the floor but winced from the effort. "You were right. They're nice."

"Told you." Noah peeked into the bathroom and marched back through the suite. "My man, Dallas Avery. It's good to meet you, man." He held his fist out for a pound. "I saw the game when you played the Raptors. Me and a few friends got tickets. You must have scored forty plus points on us."

Dallas tapped his fist to Noah's, feeling like he was watching a tennis match the way Noah was in constant motion. The boy sat in a chair but bounced up to examine the sleeping infant. Then he went to the cathedral window and observed the view. He ended up back near the counter where Jada's leftover meal rested.

"You know, I had my own little hoop dreams. I was pretty good with it, too." Noah dipped a limp French fry in ketchup.

"Why'd you stop playing?" Dallas asked leaning on the bar.

"Look at me, man." Noah wiped greasy fingers on a napkin and tossed it on the plate. "I'm what, five feet six."

Dallas laughed. He liked this kid. From Alicia's amused expression, he could tell she liked him too. "Mugsy, Spud, Isaiah, and Calvin Murphy were also shorties, but they made their mark on the sport."

Noah shrugged.

"Alright, so how about you tell us what we're into here. Jada told us about her father and the Triad. Where do you come in?" Dallas settled onto the bed beside Alicia and placed his hand on the baby's back.

Noah leaned against the counter but quickly shifted a gaze to the door. "We have to get the baby out of here. I was able to sneak Jada out of the house and stash her in an empty room here. But she went into labor, and I freaked out." He shuddered, as if remembering a sight he shouldn't have seen. "But I have connections."

Alicia peppered Noah with questions while Dallas took notes. The Triad had recruited Noah a year ago. He needed money to help his mother and five siblings, who were living in a two-bedroom apartment near Ontario. They assigned him to watch the boss's daughter since he was close enough to her age to blend in. He also ran errands as well as stole an item or two. "I'm good with my hands," he added.

"I have some people working behind the scenes," Dallas stated.

"You can't wait," Noah said, glancing out of the window again. "I managed to shake off those thugs, but they may come after my mom. Please Mr. Avery, you have to get them out of here."

Alicia handed the baby off to Dallas who placed her on his chest. She seemed smaller in his arms. She started packing their bags and motioned for Jada to put on her shoes. "Noah, you're very brave."

"I know this ain't the woman claiming she's having your baby," Noah gestured to Alicia but put his focus on Dallas. "Naw, she too classy for that."

Dallas almost dropped the toiletry bag that Alicia held out to him. "What do you know about that?"

Noah shrugged. "Saw a report online. Can't believe you got trapped, man. Thought you old dudes knew the rules. You got to wrap it up."

"Like you should have with Jada, huh?" Dallas liked this kid, but he wouldn't let him disrespect him like that.

Noah laughed and shook his head. "You think me and Jada … No way. She's like my little sister. She's too young for me. I'm sixteen, what I look like with a thirteen-year-old?"

"If you're not the daddy…" Alicia broke off her sentence when she saw Jada freeze in place, eyes wide with fear.

Noah was at the door when he glanced over his shoulder. "Naw, the baby daddy ain't me. It's her father."

Chapter 15

"I need your help," Dallas said into his phone after reaching out to the contact Alex gave him earlier.

"Tell me what you need," the caller responded in a raspy voice.

He watched Alicia as she tried to engage Jada's interest in the baby. She ignored the infant and instead held whispered conversations with Noah. Dallas couldn't really blame the girl. Having a baby by your father would taint the whole motherhood thing. The emotional pain had to be equal to the physical. Maybe with some help she could master the basic mother stuff.

Dallas walked to the door, squinting through the peep hole. "Francois, I need to get my lady, a young girl, and her friend, Noah, out of the county sooner than later. I can't tell the corrupt from the legit police. My friend, Alex, said you would know someone here that can help us."

"Stay where you are; I'll find you. Stay off the phone unless I call you. Give me one hour." With that, the call was disconnected.

Alicia joined Dallas by the door and whispered, "Dallas, how are we going to get these babies out of here?" The baby was swaddled on the bed, and the kids were debating about the latest hit from some boy band.

He pulled her into his arms, more for his comfort than hers. She seemed to be handling the situation a lot better than he was. "I'm working on it. Trust me the safety of you all is my top priority," he reassured her with a kiss to her forehead.

Dallas wanted to ask Noah and Jada more questions but didn't want to press, because the young girl had finally stopped crying. When Noah dropped the news about her father, she had shut down hard. The only one able to get the blank look from her eyes was Noah, but even his anger was palpable.

When Jada went to the bathroom, Dallas motioned Noah over. "What do you know about her mother?"

"Dead." Noah glanced over his shoulder at the closed bathroom door. "She offed herself. Rumor has it that Tony had Jada's mom from the time she was Jada's age. She was a beautiful black lady with hazel eyes. I'll always remember those eyes. They held no light."

"What do you mean no light?" Dallas asked, moving in so they were a few inches apart.

"I guess everything Tony done to her killed her on the inside first. The only thing left for her to do was take her life. He was plenty mad about it, too. Told all the guys she was weak and did it to make him look bad. Then he started in on Jada."

Alicia's green eyes flashed. "We can't let her go back to that. Her father is a monster."

"Don't worry," Dallas agreed. "We'll get them out."

He checked his watch, hoping his words would come true.

* * *

The call came an hour later. Dallas hesitated to answer the phone. Three rings and a hang up. The phone rang again; this time he answered on the fourth ring.

"Listen carefully," the caller said.

Dallas stood at the window and nodded to Alicia before putting the phone back to his ear. "Continue," he calmly said.

"I'm sending someone to pick you up. It will be my nephew, Kevin. I'll send a picture to your phone, so you know what he looks like. He is bringing things for the group. There'll be a gun in there for you. Hope you know how to use it because you'll probably need it."

It had been a while since he went to the shooting range, but he believed his skills hadn't suffered that much from lack of practice. "I can handle my own," Dallas replied.

"Once he picks you up and drops the ladies off at a spot on the Underground Railroad, he'll bring you and Noah to me. I have a friend that should have arrived by then that will be able to help further. Kevin won't call you. A message will be left at the front desk that your package has arrived. Then you leave the hotel by the emergency exit, and he'll be there waiting."

"Got it," Dallas said and disconnected the call.

"Baby, we have to get stuff prepared to leave here." He grabbed the few bags they had and placed them by the door.

Alicia bagged the baby's and Jada's things and put them with the other items. Then she picked up the baby as Noah woke Jada. He explained the situation to them, and Jada slipped on her shoes and perched on the beige comforter, while Noah held her hand.

Dallas was still floored by how young she really looked. He would love to get his hands on her slimeball father for what he'd done to her. How could a man molest his own daughter?

The room phone rang, and Dallas picked it up.

"This is Andrew at the front desk. Your package has arrived, sir."

"Thank you." Dallas replaced the phone in the cradle and motioned for everyone to head to the door. He made sure that he walked out first just in case someone had snuck into the building.

"I'll go and check around." Noah led the group down the far stairway and through the underbelly of the hotel. "I sneak in this way to see my mom sometimes. She works double, sometimes triple, shifts, and I just need to know she's all right."

Dallas dropped the bags he carried down several flights of stairs through a maintenance corridor and up to a silver metal door with a warning sign. *Do Not Exit. Alarm will sound.*

"Are you sure about this?" He gestured toward the sign.

Noah smirked. "No worries, man. I got connections."

Alicia and Jada brought up the rear. The stairs had taken a noticeable toll on Jada. She moved slowly and lowered herself onto a wooden box. "I need a minute," she panted.

"Babe," Alicia called out. "How about you guys look out for the car, and we'll wait here?" She shifted the baby from one arm to the other.

"Maybe I can carry her," Dallas said.

"No, you'll need your hands free."

"This door leads to the back alley," Noah placed his hand on the exterior door. "Your ride should be back here."

Dallas and Noah left the building and walked into a uniformed officer whose broad shoulders strained against a navy dress shirt. The bulletproof vest with POLICE across the front was as big as a billboard. "Got you," he said clapping a beefy hand on Noah's collar.

"Let him go." Dallas tried to grab for Noah's arm, but another officer rounded the corner and thrust a hand in his chest.

"Stay out of this." The second officer was shorter and had his red hair cut military style. "It's official police business."

Noah struggled to get out of the big guy's grip. "Man, I ain't do nothing."

Dallas watched the officer frisk Noah, finding a switchblade in his boot.

"We got you now, you little punk. Someone wants to talk to you." The large tank of a man dragged Noah toward a black sedan with tinted windows idling a few feet away.

"Wait, you can't take him. What are you arresting him for?" Dallas started to follow, but the shorter officer stepped in his path.

"Stay back, or I'll have to take you in, too."

Dallas sidestepped and kept going toward Noah. "You can't do this. I'm not going to let you harass this kid."

The officer spun Dallas around and placed his Glock on Dallas' temple. "Don't make me handcuff you."

Time seemed to freeze frame as Dallas stood there powerless to help. He turned to see the window on the car being lowered but was too far away to see who was inside. Whoever it was made Noah's body go stiff. Words were said, the edges of sounds not reaching Dallas' position. Noah shook his head in response.

"This kid is bad news. Do you know he kidnapped a pregnant girl? Her father is worried sick." The short officer puffed out his chest and narrowed his eyes. "Would you happen to know anything about it?"

"What girl?" Dallas stared back at the officer and prayed Jada and Alicia would stay put.

"I know who you are, Basketball Star. It's the only reason I'm going to let you go." The cop glared up at him. "But if you try to intervene or report this, we'll find you."

Noah's shouts drew his attention back to the car. He'd managed to break free of the officer's grasp and ran back toward the hotel. Dallas saw a weapon appear at the window and, without thinking, ran toward Noah. He grabbed the boy and spun him around using his own body as a shield. Shots rang out.

The cadence of bangs bounced off the concrete walls as Dallas landed on top of Noah. They rolled to a stop against a green metal trash bin and crawled around the side for protection. Dallas held Noah in place until he heard the squealing of the sedan's tires.

Gulping for oxygen, Noah pushed Dallas off. "I can't breathe, man." The smell of sulfur and metal filled the air.

"Are you hit?" Dallas asked trying to catch his own breath. "Did you get shot?" He crouched to look around the bin.

Seeing the car was gone, they both stood.

"Can't believe Tony tried to take me out." Noah wiped dust from his shoulders and then collapsed. A bloom of red appeared on his shirt.

"Noah. Man, no." Dallas checked the boy's chest and applied pressure to the wound with both hands. His eyes searched for help, but the only person around was the fallen officer who'd taken a few bullets himself. He wasn't moving.

The biggest officer who was near the sedan must have bailed along with the car. Dallas was about to call Alicia when he spotted a man who matched the description Francois had given him. "Help me."

"Leave him, he's dead." Kevin said pulling Dallas away. "There's nothing you can do for him."

"No, he can't be. I'm not leaving him on the street," Dallas yelled looking at the blood on his hands.

"I'll have it taken care of, don't worry." Kevin punched a code into his phone. "Right now, we must get out of here," Kevin assured him.

"Alicia. I have to get them from the hotel." Dallas ran back toward the building when Alicia opened the door.

"What's going on out here? It sounded like gunfire." Alicia's eyes widened when she saw the body on the street. Jada followed behind her before Dallas could answer.

"Where's Noah?" Jada's eyes frantically searched for the boy. "We can't leave Noah."

Dallas tried to shield Jada from Noah's body, but the girl became hysterical at the sight. "Please stop," Dallas pleaded. "He'll be okay, but we need to get out of here."

He sent up a silent prayer that Noah would survive.

With everyone in the car and situated, Kevin handed Dallas the special package just for him, a Sig Sauer P320 9mm.

"This should do nicely."

Chapter 16

"How is this supposed to work?" Alicia asked, trying to make eye contact with Dallas, who avoided her efforts.

"Everything will be explained later. I've got to go." He placed a chaste kiss on her cheek and jumped back in the car just before Kevin pulled away.

She walked into the entrance of the Underground Railroad, that looked like nothing more than a cave dug out of the side of a mountain. If anyone had told her coming to Canada would have given her this experience, she wouldn't have believed them. Her company was an elderly salt and pepper-haired woman, who reminded her of her grandmother.

"Baby, you just leave everything to us. We've done this before, and your safety is our only concern." Her weathered hand touched Alicia's providing just the right amount of pressure to alleviate her concerns.

"We will get you home with this precious package."

"My name is Mary, and at the next juncture you will find Martha and Esther. For now, let me check this baby out and make sure she's all right. I was a midwife back in the day and still know more than any of these young doctors. I'll give the mother a check as well."

With a wink she went about her duties and left Alicia to her thoughts.

Alicia had no way to get in touch with Dallas. Their escorts said it was best to break up the group to make it harder for someone to follow. She wasn't sure it was a good plan, but Dallas said there would be messages along the way.

Dallas was nothing like her former husband, Patrick. He wanted nothing to do with children that weren't his, but it wasn't her fault he couldn't maintain an erection longer than three minutes. He tried to make his short comings all about her, and for a while she believed him. After one night with Dallas, she knew she had never been the problem. He wanted children. At her age babies were not in her future unless he was open to adoption. Since he was a young viral male, she doubted that would be his choice, when he could have children of his own. She'd promised him a few more days, and she would keep that promise, but then this had to end before he got hurt. He was different than the ball players she saw on television. He kept his personal life private, loved his mother, and was savvy with his finances. He treated his career as a business because just like business at any given hour it could come to a crashing halt. Even with the rumors circulating, she knew he wasn't guilty of what the reporter had thrown out there. If he was, he would be there for his child. After seeing him worry about Jada and the baby, she was certain.

"Ms. Mary, can I help you with anything?" Alicia asked after she snapped back to the present.

"Her breathing is a little labored, and that has me concerned. Like maybe she has fluid in her lungs or something. I wish I had access to an ultrasound machine. I figure it may be just a cold. Rub this on her chest and keep her wrapped up." She placed a jar of salve in Alicia's hand.

"There are flannels, blankets, jackets, and other things along the route for you both and the baby. Tonight, you will be safe here. I'll be back early in the morning with food and other things to help you in getting to your next stop." Mary explained.

Alicia listened as the instructions were given. She repeated everything back to Mary while keeping a watchful eye on Jada, who was busy feeding and changing the baby.

"Ms. Mary can you get a message to someone stateside?" She pulled her jacket just a little tighter as a bit of wind whipped through the entrance of the tunnel.

"I will do my best, sweetheart. We haven't had to deliver messages in a while, but no time like the present to try." Mary winked again which seemed to be a bit of a habit.

Alicia explained, "I need to get a message to my friend, Marla. If possible, I need her to meet me at the next stop. If she's there, I'll know the message got through."

Marla and Alicia had reconnected recently. They had been friends since both had grown up in the system. She had kept tabs on Marla for years and welcomed the woman who had embraced her as family from the beginning. As good as Alicia was with a blade, Marla was even better. She had taught Alicia most of what she knew.

"Don't worry. I'll get it to her," Mary answered Alicia by pulling her into a hug. "Now rest. See you in the morning."

Alicia looked around the tunnel and marveled at the brick work. There were barrels and crates stacked along the smooth limestone walls, as she walked with Mary back to the entrance. "I won't rest until this is over."

She settled in around Jada, who was fast asleep. After checking the baby, she whispered a prayer for all of them. "God, please let us make it home."

Chapter 11

"This is not your fight," Francois explained to Dallas, who had been ranting since Noah was shot, and it seemed no one cared.

"Someone has to right the wrong done to these people," Dallas replied. They had driven for an hour before Kevin pulled into what looked like an abandoned building, but it turned out to be much more than that. He didn't know everything they were into, but with all the high-tech equipment in the building it looked like a full-scale military operation. These people were helping him and Alicia return to the States with Jada and the baby under the radar. That was all that mattered.

"I called some guys I know, and they picked Noah up and took him to the hospital. They also notified his mother, and she and his siblings are with him. Now can we get down to business?"

"When will we know his condition? I'll cover his hospital bills. I don't want his mom worry about his care." Dallas said a silent prayer for Noah's family, especially his mother. He wouldn't ever wish anything like this on his.

"We got it covered. They're all safe at an undisclosed location," Kevin said while opening the door. The buzzer had been going off for a second.

Dallas would swear that El Debarge's brother had just walked in the door. Kevin escorted the gentleman over. "Alejandro Reyes, this is Dallas Avery."

He stood and extended his hand. Based on quick intel he got from Kevin, Alejandro was a member of a group of brothers known as 'The Kings'. Each man has their own territory in the Chicago area. Alejandro was known as the King of Hyde Park. "Please to meet you, Sir."

"Sir is my father. I'm just Dro," he said, taking Dallas' hand in his. "Nice to meet you, man. You have mad skills on the basketball court."

Dallas gave him a warm smile.

"Okay, let's get this show on the road." Francois motioned for each man to join him at the computer he sat in front of. He explained everything they had been doing over the past year. Surveillance videos of Tony Soto's operation were playing on the big screen. Images of young girls being drugged, beaten, and worse.

"If you have all of this information on this guy, why haven't you taken him down or at least turned him over to the police?" Dallas questioned, not fully understanding why they were dragging the man's judgement out.

"Because they are very intertwined within the Soto organization. It's hard to tell who's legit and who's not," Kevin answered. "When we take them down, we'd like to take everyone."

Dallas studied the man in the horn-rimmed glasses, who looked like the computer geek type.

"I'm an ex-marine, and we work from the top down. The best way to kill a snake is to cut it off at the head."

Dro took in all of the information and snapped a few pictures with his phone. "Can you bring up a picture of the house and his business location?"

With a couple clicks on the keyboard, the pictures were up. Dro wasted no time capturing them and hitting send on his phone.

"Here's what will happen. By tomorrow morning all his business entities will be hit. All the corrupt police will be removed, and everyone associated with Mr. Soto will disappear. My team will strike all locations at once.

"Do I even want to know what all this entails?" Dallas asked.

The corner of Alejandro's mouth lifted in a smile, but it was devoid of any warmth. "Nope, you don't. Kevin will drop you at the next location to meet your lady. There'll be a few people from my organization watching her and the girl travel through the tunnels. Keep your piece on you at all times. Got it?"

"Yes. I got it," Dallas responded.

"Let's do it." Francois powered off all the equipment and locked up as they left.

Dallas walked toward the car with Kevin. "Man, I don't know if my woman will travel with me anywhere else after this one."

"Why wouldn't she?" Kevin asked.

Dallas closed the door once seated, "I can always ask for one more day."

Chapter 18

"Thanks for bringing the knives." Alicia embraced Marla. "After seeing how these guys operate, I need to be able to protect myself."

Marla rolled out an assortment of blades, daggers, two swords, short blade pocketknives, and a few Alicia could hide in a pair of combat boots that she brought. "You know how this works. Protect yourself at all costs."

She remembered. When Mr. Barkley from the foster home tried to have his way, Marla made sure he would always remember when he unzipped his pants. Let's just say Lorena Bobbitt wasn't the first woman to cut one off. Marla was sent away from the foster home after that, but no one would dare mess with her either.

"I'll cover myself and the babies, without question." Alicia replaced her shoes with the boots and slid the knives in the special slots as instructed. "Are you leaving out today?"

"No ma'am, I'm here with you until you cross the border. Ain't no way I'd let you have all this fun without me. Lucky for you I was in Detroit on business, and I always carry my credentials." Marla tossed a backpack over her shoulder and grabbed the baby's bag. "Now let's get going."

"Jada, you ready?"

Alicia and Marla turned and waited for her to pick up the baby.

"Yes," she replied, wrapping the baby in the blanket Mary had provided and catching up with them.

"Wait one second ladies," Mary's soft voice echoed in the tunnel. She pulled out some tan parchment paper that looked like a scroll, "This will help guide your way, and maybe a few spirituals, too. Be safe and stay on the path."

Alicia hugged Mary tight, inhaling the scent of cinnamon and vanilla. "Thank you so much." One last touch of their hands, and they were on their way.

Forever taking the lead, Marla grabbed the scroll, while Alicia took the baby from Jada and handed her a bag. The tunnels were illuminated somewhat, so they could see a few feet at a time.

"I'm tired," Jada proclaimed after they had walked nearly three hours. "Can we rest for a minute, so I can feed the baby."

Alicia smiled glad to see her taking an interest in the well-being of the baby. "You really need to give her a name. We can't just keep calling her the baby." She looked down at the infant and was rewarded with a toothless grin and the prettiest dimples she'd ever seen.

"I can't think of anything. Maybe she shouldn't have a name until she makes it to her new family."

Marla stepped in front of Jada. "Everyone deserves a name. Even dogs have names. She is beautiful and needs a name. If she is adopted and they decide to change her name, she will always be to you the name you assigned at her birth."

She placed her hand on Jada's shoulder then stepped away.

"Desirée Noelle," Jada replied. Her eyes darting between both ladies, "Desirée was my mom's name, and Noelle to honor Noah for helping me." Tears fell like raindrops from her eyes. "I hope Noah is okay."

Alicia walked over to where Jada sat on a section of the tunnel that was carved to resemble a bench. "Don't cry. Everything's going to be just fine. We'll make it across the border."

Jada wiped her eyes with the back of her glove. "I'm not crying because I'm scared. I've lost everyone and everything I cared about: my mom, my best friend, and my virginity to a father who was supposed to protect me. Why did he hurt me?"

Alicia squeezed her hand. "Some men just aren't meant to be fathers. That doesn't justify what he did. He was wrong and believe me he will be sorry he ever touched you in that way." She allowed Jada to cry on her shoulder for a few minutes longer.

"We have to move." Marla returned to where they were standing. "There's some movement back the way we came."

Alicia grabbed the baby and a backpack. Jada and Marla picked up everything else. They moved at a steady pace through the tunnels for another hour before stopping. She pulled out the parchment that Mary had given her.

"There's a place for us to hide and rest up above. If something jumps off, Jada and the baby will be safe there. Let's go."

They climbed down inside another cave, hidden by a rock. Inside were a few places to sit that have been etched out of the wall, lanterns, food, and more blankets. "Jada, can you change the baby and feed her? Maybe give Desirée a wash up if you can. When we come back in, I'll rub some more salve on your chest, and then we rest."

"Yes, ma'am." Jada picked up the baby and did as Alicia instructed.

"Let's go see who is crazy enough to try and track us down," Marla said with a laugh. They both grabbed an extra blade from the bag. Alicia turned back and handed one along with the document to Jada. "If we don't make it back, follow this to find your way." She pointed at a spot on the parchment. "We're here, and you need to go about three more hours to reach New York. There'll be two ladies named Esther and Martha waiting with a car."

Jada scrounged around in her backpack and produced some paperwork. "If we go through security, won't I need these?" She handed both her school id and passport to Alicia.

"No, you won't need these. Esther will have new documents for you to travel with should you need them. You'll be in a private hanger where they usually don't ask for id." Marla took the liberty of breaking everything down.

"If we aren't back in an hour, tomorrow morning you start out. Got it?"

"I don't want to leave without you," Jada cried. "Please don't make me stay here."

Alicia touched her cheek and turned her head to the baby, "For her, you have to do this. There is more at stake now besides you. She comes first. She needs you. Got it."

Jada straightened her back and dried her tears. "I can do this, for her."

"Good." Alicia and Marla went back out of the cave the way they entered.

"I think she's going to make it now that you're in her corner."

Alicia glanced at her friend. "Why do you say that? She'll make it whether I'm there or not. She has a reason to."

"No." Marla shook her head. "You gave her a reason to. She gave birth to the baby, but from what I've been hearing she is just ready to be done with it."

"You're so wrong. Yes, she was ready to give the baby away, but it was to protect her. That has always been her priority, to get the baby to safety. She acted unselfishly, and that is a maternal instinct. She just needed to remember why she did. I know she's hurting and confused, but she will protect that baby at all costs."

Sounds of guns being cocked reached their ears way before trouble stepped in front of them. Alicia remembered seeing a little hiding place just ahead. Both ducked in and were hidden as two guys walked by with semi-automatics. Marla was first to attack the guy in behind. She slit his throat before he could make a peep. Before the second could turn around, Alicia had picked up the first one's gun and shot him.

"I think we should wait a minute to make sure there's no one else," Alicia whispered as she placed the gun on the ground.

"We're keeping the weapons, and I'm sure there will be more once these two don't return. Hopefully, that will put us hours ahead of them. 'Cause whoever's outside is just a driver, and they'll need to return or wait there for some other guys to come. My guess is he'll go pick them up, and there'll be a lot more of them." Marla stared at Alicia for a long time.

"What? Why are you staring at me?" Alicia asked.

Marla laughed for a minute. "You did good back there, but your face when you saw his neck. If I wasn't busy, I would've smacked you."

Their laughter was interrupted by the loud cries of the baby. "We got to hurry." Alicia screamed as they both ran in the direction of the cries.

"Shut that crying baby up." The husky voice said. "You should've just stayed and let Tony take the baby. Wait until he gets his hands on you."

Marla put her forefinger to her lip as they both tipped closer to cave. The rock had been removed. "Here I thought cowards didn't play at night. These men are crazy," she whispered.

"Tony will kill you if you hurt the baby or me. I'll tell him everything you said about slitting my throat," Jada screamed, "let me go Rio."

Alicia ran in, gun forgotten, "Leave her alone." She shouted, raising her hands in the air as the gun held by a second guy swung in her direction.

The big burly guy, Rio, held Jada by her hair, and the other well-dressed one held a gun.

"We've been waiting for you. Both of you are coming with us, Tiny, keep the gun on that one."

Alicia turned to exit the same way she entered, but not before grabbing the backpack sitting close to the entrance, followed by the gun holder. Jada and the baby were behind them followed by the obvious leader of the group. Alicia didn't see Marla but knew her friend overheard everything that was said.

The gun in her back forced Alicia to move; she walked the narrow, pebbled path in the tunnel. The temperature was dropping, and she worried the baby would get sick. As if on cue, little Desireé began to cry again. "Let me take her and see if I can get her quiet." Alicia tossed over her shoulder.

"Hurry up and you'd better not try anything," the smaller assailant named Tiny responded.

Alicia assured Jada everything would be fine, then she tended to the baby and bundled her up. She handed the baby back to Jada with care and whispered in her ear, "When I tell you to, take the baby and run as fast as you can." Then holding Jada's hand, they walked to the front of the line and continued through the tunnels. Alicia made sure to position Jada where neither she nor the baby would be injured when something jumped off. The temperature was cool, but the eerie silence, other than the creatures that roam in the dark, was her clue that Marla was waiting ahead for them.

"It's getting colder, and I'm really tired. Can't we rest?" Jada's face appeared even more ashen in the dim light.

"There is no stopping. We have no more time to for stalling. Either you walk or I'll carry you". Rio moved in her direction. "It's your choice."

"Never mind, creep," Jada mumbled under her breath.

Alicia reached into the backpack and pulled out two blankets. One for the baby and one to wrap around Jada. "Here that should keep you warm," she said placing one around Jada's shoulders. She swaddled the baby in the second one. Secretly, she prayed that they didn't have much further to go. Alicia was pretty sure that was a short cut ahead and hoped these two knew that way. The sooner they were out of the tunnel with them the better, so they could escape.

They walked another forty minutes, maybe less. Alicia was uncertain of the time because between the baby and helping Jada stay on her feet, she was getting tired as well.

"Turn here," Rio yelled from the rear. "It's a short cut. We'll reach your destination faster." His nervous laughter echoed throughout the tunnels.

Alicia halted her footsteps, "What do you mean my destination?"

Tiny nudged her with the butt of the gun, but she didn't budge. Alicia stood firm with her hands on her hips.

"We only came for the baby; our instructions are to kill you and the girl and leave you in the tunnel," Rio responded.

"Well, if that's the case you might as well do that here and take the baby." Alicia pulled Jada's trembling frame closer to her. "I'm sure if you don't make it to Tony with the crying baby, you will meet the same fate as we did, if not worse." Alicia formulated a plan to buy some time. "Take both of us closer to the end of the tunnel then you can do as you please with me, but you will need her to keep the baby quiet until you reach Tony."

"I'm not going with them," Jada's head snapped toward Alicia. "I can't go back there."

She looked down at Desireé's sleeping face. Why would anyone want to sell such a precious infant? Alicia already knew the answer, to hide the sins of the father. Nobody was dying in this tunnel today. Well, neither her, Jada, nor the baby. She couldn't speak for these two goons.

"It's okay, baby, they aren't going to hurt you," Alicia held Jada by the shoulders and starred in her eyes. "You will be all right. Understand?"

"Yes, ma'am."

"Enough," Rio yelled. "Tiny, go in front. We'll keep them between us."

They walked for another twenty minutes before Alicia handed the baby off to Jada. "Protect her at all costs," she whispered. She turned at the sound of a loud thud, pushing Jada and Desireé out of the way. She knew Marla hadn't left and was just waiting for an opportune moment. For a split second she forgot about Tiny ahead of them with the gun; he was still walking. Alicia tipped behind him. What idiot put earbuds in when trying to kidnap someone? Alicia hit Tiny with a karate chop to the side of his neck. He dropped faster than a hooker's panties. Now she could concentrate on helping Marla with Rio.

Marla doubled over from the punch he landed in her mid-section. Alicia ran and did a heel kick to his knee, but not before he landed a punch to her arm. She shook off the punch and did a roundhouse to his jaw that only seemed to stun him. Alicia was thankful for those karate lessons over the years. As Rio started to return to a standing position, both ladies, hit him with a front kick, a roundhouse, and then a back kick that leveled him.

Jada stood off to the side clutching the baby to her chest, mouth hung open wide. This looked like a scene from a mixed martial arts tournament to her.

"Enough," Marla yelled as Rio got up again, ready to storm at them.

"No, Jada," Alicia screamed.

Rio turned around and put his hands up. "You wouldn't shoot me little girl. You're a coward just like your mother."

Bullets ripped through his body, until he fell as Jada emptied the clip into him. "I'm not a coward and neither was my mother." She dropped the gun and clutched the baby again.

Alicia ran and wrapped her up in her arms. "No baby, you're definitely not a coward."

Even Marla embraced Jada for that one. "Good looking out, little bit."

Thirty minutes later, after wading through mucky water and overgrown bushes, and ducking a bat or two they reached their destination. As promised two ladies, who appeared to be in their late eighty's met them with a SUV. Alicia and Marla loaded everything while Jada got in the vehicle. Once everyone was settled and introductions made, they were off.

Martha, the younger of the two sisters was at the wheel. "We're taking you straight to the airport. There's a private plane waiting to take you to Chicago."

"Back when the railroad was in full operation, you would've been in a wagon or on the train or continuing the journey by foot. Thank God for modern transportation." She reached in her purse and pulled out an envelope. "Don't open this until you're on the plane."

After a thirty-minute ride, with Marla yelling for Jada to duck when a car passed, they pulled onto the private airstrip.

"Thank you, ladies, for helping us."

"It was our pleasure," Martha replied.

Esther patted Alicia's hand. "Honey, I haven't been this excited since my husband left this earth. This was a wonderful adventure. Now get on that plane."

Chapter 19

"How did you get him?" Dallas stood stunned as they dragged the man identified as Tony Soto in the building. "Is he dead?"

Francois and Dro placed him in an iron chair that sat against the wall. "No, he's just drugged. He'll come around in a few. Then he'll wish we had killed him."

Dallas had been antsy since he returned to the warehouse. Constantly pacing the tattered wooden floor because he was worried about Alicia and Jada.

"Man, can you please stop that?" Kevin shook his head and stepped in his path. "Your woman is fine. The girl and baby are fine. They will meet you in Chicago."

A slow smile slid across Dallas' face as he sighed with relief. "I knew she would make it." He jumped like he did on his last slam dunk. "Alright. Now I can concentrate on this slimeball." He pushed up his sleeves, ready for action.

"No, you can't. You're on the next flight out of here to Chicago. Grab your things so Kevin can run you to the airport." Alejandro made his way from the side of the room where he was handcuffing Tony to the seat. "We got it from here. Go take care of your woman. Besides, that little girl needs you guys right now. It's not about him." He pointed his long finger at Tony. "His entire network has more children and women caught up in it. Someone will call you when everything's been resolved."

Dallas complied, feeling dismissed and disappointed. He wanted to rearrange Tony's face for Jada and for Noah. He held his hand out to Dro and waited only seconds before it was accepted along with a pat on the back and repeated the same for Francois. "Thanks, guys. I appreciate all you've done to helps us. I hate to think what would've happened without you."

"No problem, that's what we do," Francois responded with a smile.

On the drive, Kevin shared with Dallas that he was a troubled kid as a teenager, and Francois had helped him out. Gave him a job, sent him to school, and kept him employed while he was in college. In the summers he would help guiding tours. They spearheaded fixing the tunnels used in the Underground Railroad to enhance the experience for tourists.

"So, they used the tunnels to get out of Canada? How'd they know where to go?" Dallas' curiosity was piqued now.

Kevin nodded while keeping his eyes on the road. "Yes, we still have conductors that are along the way. Some of them are descendants of the original conductors, but I'm sure Alicia will tell you all about that."

"For real, they have to be like a hundred years old by now. That's amazing."

Dallas watched as Kevin steered around the back of the airport to where the private planes and jets were. They exchanged numbers before stepping out of the car.

"I have to know," Dallas closed the passenger door. "What happens to Tony? That man can't be allowed to hurt his daughter ever again."

Kevin's nostril flared. "Don't worry. Once we extract all the information about his organization, he'll be six feet under."

Dallas nodded. He would rest easy knowing Jada was free from her father. "Alright, let me get out of here."

"Go get your woman, man." Kevin turned and opened the vehicle door.

Dallas paused. "I'll keep asking for one more day 'til I win her over."

Chapter 20

Dallas stood on the tarmac at the Signature Flight Support Airport in Chicago and watched his heart descend from the clouds. The closer the plane carrying Alicia came to the ground, the easier it was for him to breath.

"Don't worry, my friend," Alex clapped him on the back. "Everything worked with only a few hiccups. Your lady is safe and sound back in the States."

"I can't thank you enough." Dallas turned and offered his hand. He hadn't seen the man in months, but the same lanky Atlanta detective flew in to meet him at the private airstrip that was part of Chicago Midway Airport. Alex really came through for him. Steering him to an honest contact in Kevin was only the beginning. The accompanying row of official vehicles and swarming U.S. Custom & Border Protection officers proved Alex had gone above and beyond.

Alex flicked away Dallas' hand and brought him in for a hug. "What you and your lady did is pretty courageous. Not many people would get involved with a stranger's problem."

"Well, when it's a kid in danger…" Dallas returned the physical greeting with two pounds to Alex's back. He stepped away and watched the plane taxi to a stop.

"How could someone try to sell a baby?" Alex fiddled with the radio on his hip. "Although I can understand being desperate enough to purchase one, but do people know the story of how it all happened?"

Dallas winced. He was so focused on his own situation he forgot to inquire about his friend's dilemma. "You can't give up, you know. It'll happen for you."

Alex squared his shoulders. "The wife's still praying. She believes we'll be blessed with a baby this year. I'm thinking it just isn't in the cards for me, but don't want to crush her hopes."

Dallas knew Alex's past history. His first wife turned out to be a real piece of work. The guy could probably write a book about his escape from that situation. He told Dallas his current wife, Daisha, had saved his life. They'd been trying for a baby for a couple of years.

The plane door opened, and Alicia appeared at the top of the stairs. She covered the baby she was holding in her arms, protecting it from the Chicago wind. She scanned the field of faces until she found his. Her smile was so bright he no longer felt the chill bite of the wind. Jada peered out from behind her and waved.

"Have you guys thought about adopting?" Dallas asked Alex, waving back as they made their way down the stairs. "That baby will need a loving family."

Alex's brow knitted. "What are you saying?"

"I'm saying, maybe the miracle you're looking for is right here." Dallas reached for Alicia's hand and pulled her into a firm embrace. He sought her lips and relished the taste and feel of her being beside him again.

Alex cleared his throat, and Jada giggled causing Dallas to step away and wink at the teen. "Sorry about that," he said. "Let me introduce you."

Alicia thanked Alex for his help. "Seems as if you brought out all the alphabet agencies," she said smiling.

"Anything to help Dallas." Alex motioned to a woman in a navy pantsuit hovering off to the side. "I was able to expedite your case. Jada and the baby will receive the full protection of the U.S. Government. Mrs. Frasier is with Children Services. She will walk you through the next steps."

Mrs. Frasier flashed a badge and knelt in front of Jada. The silver bangles on her arm jingled as she balanced a tablet in one hand. "Welcome to America, Jada. You're one brave little girl."

Jada nodded, but her gaze lowered to her feet.

"How about I come with you to get settled?" Alicia put an arm around Jada, and the girl smiled up at her.

The group followed Mrs. Frasier into the terminal and an adjacent conference room. The area had been commandeered by the agency. "Excuse me for one second; I need to retrieve something from my office." Mrs. Frasier retreated from the group.

A command center was housed on one end of the wooden table with laptops and cell phones. A flat screen television hung on the wall primed for a video discussion. Jada was ushered into a tan leather chair and offered her choice of water, juice, soda, and other assorted snacks. Alicia sat beside her and calmed the baby which had started to cry from all the activity.

"Noah!" Jada squealed, when the door to the conference room opened. "How'd you get here?" He walked in scanning the area with his mom directly behind him, while Jada pulled him in a hug.

"Easy, baby girl, the arm's still a little tender." Noah wrapped his other arm around her as Dallas and Alicia joined them.

They pulled him into an embrace. "Man, how'd you get here? I didn't want to leave you out there and not know what was happening. I was so pissed." Dallas could feel his pressure rising again just thinking about it. He embraced him again with Alicia.

"We landed right behind their plane, but I asked to be brought in a different way to surprise you. You know I got to make an entrance," he laughed.

"Let me introduce you guys to my mother, Noelle," Noah pulled his mom around. She had stood off to the side watching the reunion.

"Thank you for saving my most precious gift. I am forever in your debt." Noelle bowed her head to Dallas and Alicia.

She was wrapped in Alicia's arms. "That debt is paid in full."

Mrs. Frasier returned with Kleenex for the entire emotional group.

Dallas pulled Alex to the side. "So, what happens now?"

"We'll take her statement." Alex removed his sunglasses and hooked them on his polo shirt. "Our counterparts in Canada would love any intel she can give on her father. They have already talked with Noah."

"What happens to the baby?" Dallas tilted his head toward the table. "Jada is in no shape to be a mother. She wants to put the baby up for adoption. Maybe it can be an open one so she can see the baby later if she chooses. Or if the baby wants to contact her when she reaches eighteen, that would be possible. I've already contacted a boarding school in Texas for her. She can get some therapy, complete her education, and get back to being a kid. Maybe have some semblance of a normal life without the baby as a constant reminder. She needs time to process what she went through."

Alex shrugged. "If that's the case, the baby will probably go into foster care until then."

"Remember outside when I mentioned miracles." Dallas mimed dunking a basketball into the trash can at their feet. He watched Alex make the mental calculations in his head before continuing. "That baby needs a family. And I know a family who wants a baby."

Alex broke into a wide grin and pulled out his cell phone. "I see what you're saying. Let me make some calls and work with Mrs. Frasier. If it's something Jada wants."

Dallas snagged the lone remaining chair and sank into it. Fatigue settled over him, and he took a deep cleansing breath. The last few hours had been draining. The only thing he wanted now was his woman, a meal, and a massage.

As if reading his thoughts, Alicia passed the baby to a uniformed agent and slid onto his lap. "Are you okay?" she asked. Her hands found the tense muscles on the back of his neck and squeezed.

He pulled her closer and took in her scent. Her usual fragrance mixed with a hint of baby powder.

"I am now." They sat in silence for a beat, content to watch the activity swirl around them.

"Another adventure is in the books," Dallas said.

Alicia rested her head on his shoulder and stifled a yawn. "You know how to show a girl a good time."

He stroked her hair. "I do my best. I have to tell you what happened to Jada's father."

"And I have to tell you about our journey through the tunnel. I met up with an old friend." Alicia checked her vibrating phone. "She just landed back home in South Carolina. Marla helped me protect the girls."

Dallas marveled at the strength of this woman. He knew he was blessed and thought for the hundredth time about how perfect they were together. But he also knew it was too soon to express the depth of his passion for her. He saw marriage and babies in their future. Dallas knew she wasn't ready for that conversation.

Instead, he asked if she was ready to go home.

"Baby, I'll follow you anywhere," she whispered.

Chapter 21

"Dallas, we found her." Katie's voice came through the phone. "The lady claiming she was pregnant by you was also your waitress at Wolfgang Puck's restaurant."

Alicia and Dallas were relaxing on the sofa when the call came in. "What? How is that even possible?" He covered the phone and repeated everything to Alicia so she would know what was going on.

"Katie, I'm putting you on speakerphone so Alicia can hear this." Alicia tilted her head.

"Jessica was at the auction. She was pissed when you walked by her to meet Alicia and didn't even acknowledge her."

"But I don't even know this girl." Dallas searched his memory and had no recollection of her. "The only place I saw her was at the restaurant."

The tapping of her heels could be heard through the phone. "Where are you now?" Dallas asked.

"I'm leaving the police station," Katie responded. "She's being charged with defamation of character and blackmail. She had a load of material that was sent to us trying to blackmail you."

"What about the pregnancy?" Alicia asked. "Was she really pregnant?"

"Oh, she was full with child, but just not your seed."

They heard the car door close and the engine start.

"Sorry, I have to be back at the office in thirty minutes. Little Miss Jessica's boyfriend knocked her up and left her alone. She saw the auction and spent the last of her money to bid on you. Her thoughts were that she could sleep with you that night, and you would believe the baby was yours."

Alicia sighed. "What is wrong with the young girls of this world that when they're hurt by one man their immediate response is to try and destroy someone else? When did owning up to your responsibility and having some self-respect stop being a priority?"

"Alicia, Jessica was raised in a two-parent household but is an only child," Katie said. The only thing wrong with her is that she's selfish and spoiled. Except now, her parents aren't bailing her out because they happen to be fans of Dallas' and know you're a standup guy. They weren't happy about the guy she was dating and know she's lying. She'll be in court tomorrow at ten for her first appearance if you want to attend."

Dallas glanced at Alicia before he responded, "What will happen to her?"

"She could pay a fine of up to three thousand dollars and do one year in prison. Small compared to the damage this could've had on your career."

He stood and grabbed two bottles of water from the fridge. "Can't we just have her do therapy and community service work instead of prison? Everyone makes mistakes, but I don't want this to ruin her life." He handed Alicia a bottle and rejoined her on the sofa.

"But she was about to ruin yours, and personally, I don't think a year in prison would ruin her life. It may save her, and therapy may be even better."

Alicia nodded in agreement. "You can't let her get away with this. She'll only chose another target next time."

Dallas thought about the potential damage this girl's claim could have done. He was lucky none of his sponsors took these allegations seriously, or it could have ruined his financial prospects along with his reputation.

"Katie, I won't come to the courthouse. Let me amend what I want for her. Have my attorney tell the DA we want two years in prison, one year of probation, and two years of mandatory therapy." Dallas felt that arrangement would be fair.

"I'll see what we can do. Now get off the phone. Don't you have another trip coming up?" Katie's infectious laughter lightened the mood instantaneously.

"We're here for a day or two before we head back out," Dallas said.

"Alright boss," Katie said. "Alicia, take care of this guy, please."

Dallas ended the call and pulled Alicia closer. "Yes, please take care of me, baby."

She put her finger over his mouth as he tried to kiss her. "No wonder everyone loves you so much." Alicia kissed him.

Alicia's admiration for Dallas grew these past two week. He was committed to ensuring Noah and his mom returned to Canada. And when Jada decided she wanted to go home as well, Dallas used his influence and money to secure a guardianship placement with Noah's family. He also paid tuition for both teenagers at a private school there. The baby was being fostered by Alex and his wife. They're on track for an open adoption leaving room for Jada to meet her daughter when she comes of age.

"Promise me another day, I have more to show you," Dallas whispered.

Alicia sat back for a minute. "Let me think, for a moment." She counted the seconds on her watch. "I'm going to need a little less drama, and I'll consider giving you another day."

He leaned in to kiss her again, "Woman, you drive a hard bargain."

"Then I promise to consider one more day."

Anita L Roseboro, is a National Bestselling author. Her works include 'Summer Breeze', and 'Show Me No Mercy', and co-write of 'Knight of Grand Crossing' with Hiram 'Shogun' Harris, and poetry featured in various anthologies. A native of North Carolina, Anita is an avid fan of crime dramas, and looks forward to penning novels of the same variety. She has been a regular contributor to Naleighna Kai's Literary Café Magazine. She is currently working on Vindicated.

www.anitalroseboro.com

Sociotap https://sociatap.com/anitalroseboro

Michelle D. Rayford is a National Best-selling author whose pen sharpens spine-tingling tales of betrayal, lies, consequences… and their fallout when the truth comes out. Fitting for her brand of literary inspiration–shining the light in the darkness of deceit. Her debut novel, *Moment of Truth*, has been applauded for its real-life characters and contemporary issues and she has short stories penned in several anthologies. Michelle lives in a Southern city with her husband and two daughters and can be reached via her website at www.michelledrayford.com.

About the Days of Pleasure Series
9 Books * All Standalones * No Cliffhangers

10 Days of Pleasure

Some relationships are made in the storm. Real love survives them. Basketball star Dallas Avery has the world in the palm of his hand and a lifetime of happiness or despair within his grasp. For accomplished businesswoman, Alicia Mitchell, love is a double-edged sword wrought with happiness and pain. Business calls the soulmates to Scotland but a new, more treacherous storm is brewing back home. Can their love weather this latest test, or will a crueler fate prevail?

20 Days of Pleasure

NBA star Dallas Avery has one intention when he visits the most romantic city in the world—win Alicia Mitchell by any means necessary. They relish their time as a couple—free to explore their magnetic connection in Paris and savor the array of pleasures they discover as soul mates.

But family, friends, the media, and society at large, have various opinions about their complicated relationship. Will Dallas and Alicia find a way to stay together, or will the many factors working against them shatter their once-in-a-lifetime romance?

30 Days of Pleasure

Every end is supposed to be a beginning. After the death of her husband, Alicia Mitchell set herself up financially to embrace freedom and see the world. Then she met a detour. Until NBA basketball star Dallas Avery wrapped his arms around her, Alicia didn't know what it felt like to be cherished. Now he's drawing her focus and shifting her priorities. And Alicia doesn't mind. However, there's a shadow creeping from the edges of her dating history.

Taric Hasan, a man she considered dating until she experienced his dark side, has emerged. Although she once managed to escape him, Taric isn't done with her. He's intent on ending their relationship on his terms … with her death.

40 Days of Pleasure

The NBA's sexy and most valuable player Dallas Avery meets the beautiful Alicia Mitchell, who has one thing on her mind: leaving. Their attraction is intense, but the timing is off. Dallas is determined to convince Alicia to give their May-December relationship a chance, but when their romantic trip to the Caribbean gets derailed by them being embroiled in a local family's deadly drama, romance gets put on the back burner.

50 Days of Pleasure

When an obsessive fan threatens to derail Basketball Superstar Dallas Avery's relationship with the alluring and independent Alicia Mitchell, a trip to Canada comes at the opportune time. The historic sites and chilly landscapes help to stir the growing connection between the couple.

Then a distressed infant is thrust into their care. The teenage mother and her baby are in danger and only trust Dallas and Alicia to help. With the local mob in pursuit and Dallas and Alicia unable to depend on the police, they must flee the country using a historic mode of escape.

60 Days of Pleasure

Determined to give Alicia Mitchell the love that she longs for, NBA-star Dallas Avery whisks her away on exciting adventures around the world.

Dallas let his heart dictate their journey to Seattle and allows the Emerald City to work its magic on Alicia. Until civil unrest involving the indigenous people collides with a dirty politician's plans to use city funds to cover personal debts. A chance meeting with Yuma, a tribal chief's son, creates an opportunity for Dallas to make a difference for those whose voices have been silenced. When an altercation with the police develops after Dallas and Alicia assist a homeless woman, Yuma's tribe is forced to shift gears and protect the couple.

Can Dallas keep the love of his life safe, and will the civil unrest drive a permanent wedge between them?

Dallas Avery and Alicia Mitchell are off to Nashville, Tennessee for business and pleasure. Unfortunately, the past returns to haunt the basketball superstar and puts both in imminent danger.

Conway Ackerman has spent the last five years in prison, charged with aggravated stalking of the athlete early in his career. A bitter man with a sordid past, and a psychotic personality, Ackerman has recently been let out of prison and has set a course that will exact the perfect revenge.

While Dallas is aware of the convict's release, he keeps Alicia in the dark. The stage is set for a myriad of adventures, which will extend to the iconic Beale Street in Memphis, but danger is in the midst. A race against time ensues as the couple is tracked from place to place. Will they survive or meet their demise at the hands of a man whose mental state is deadly?

80 Days of Pleasure

From a romantic picnic in the Southwest to jet-setting around the globe to exotic destinations, Dallas Avery lays the foundation for a long-lasting relationship with Alicia Mitchell, brick by brick, beginning with these five words, "Just one more day, baby."

While traveling the romantic countryside from Munich, Germany to Schloss Neuschwanstein, a case of mistaken identity threatens their freedom and possibly their lives. Dallas has faced numerous threats, but nothing could have prepared him for this experience. A desire to make Alicia's childhood dream come true has evolved into an incredible nightmare.

Dallas and Alicia struggle to learn the new rules of engagement they have been forced to play by. One thing is certain, the NBA player is determined they will not be on the losing end.

90 Days of Pleasure

Alicia Mitchell, is and was, the only woman Dallas Avery has ever loved. He strives to soothe her fears about their age difference, the unresolved issues of her past, and is determined to make her his forever.

An impromptu trip to Durabia brings more danger to their relationship. Crown Prince Amir sets his sights on Alicia and puts a diabolical plan in motion for her to be secretly brought into the palace where he can have her all to himself. None of them could fathom that a third party would intervene, and plunge Dallas and Alicia in the middle of a brotherly war.

USA TODAY Bestselling Author, Naleighna Kai, tells the dynamic love triangle of a chance encounter that lands wealthy NBA star, Dallas Avery, back in the arms of Alicia, the woman of his dreams. A woman he hasn't seen in years. A woman he soon discovers is his fiancée's long-lost aunt!

But Tori, isn't ready to give up all that she's worked for in their relationship, so she makes him a shocking offer—go through with the wedding and she'll still allow him to be with the one woman he now can't seem to do without. Dallas will get a family, something her aunt can't give him and Tori will have the lifestyle she clamors. And Alicia will embrace the love she's longed for all her life and that had already been in her reach before she disappeared. Everyone will get a little of what they want. . . and maybe a whole lot of what they don't.

The details of the trio's love life play out in the tabloids and on talk shows, making Dallas the center of an NBA scandal. Eventually, the doors slam shut on this open marriage in the making and Dallas is forced to make a choice to end the chaos.

Chapter 1

Cedar Crest Inn
Asheville, NC

Fueled by adrenaline, Casey staggered out of the bedroom, and inched down the stairs to the main lobby. She almost made it to the door when a woman's voice stopped her.

"Wait, are you okay?"

Casey looked over her shoulder. The silver-haired hostess, Mrs. Harper, was standing near the front desk holding a cup of tea; worry etched in the lines across her face. "Can I help you?"

"Where's the hospital?" Casey asked, unable to keep the tremors from her voice.

"About a mile down the road."

Casey nodded and moved toward the door.

"You didn't say no or stop ... how is it rape?" he said.

"Honey, it's snowing outside," Mrs. Harper warned, causing Casey to glance at her as she placed the cup on the counter and rounded the desk. "You can't go out in just a comforter and no shoes. Let me help you."

"No," Casey protested recoiling. The last thing she wanted was for this woman, who'd been so kind since they arrived, to know what her husband had done. "I'm fine," she lied, knowing that was far from the truth.

"You're my wife ... I love you," he said. "How can you think I'd rape you?"

She tipped out of the inn's front door. Her only protection from the freezing temperature was the tan comforter draped around her body. She didn't feel the snow on her bare feet and somehow managed to coordinate her limbs enough to make it to the car. Casey unlocked the door and tried to slide behind the wheel. Nothing could have prepared her for the searing pain that hit when she attempted to sit down. Crying out, she immediately shifted her weight until she was lying on her side across the seat.

Casey tried to summon the strength to get herself to safety, but the adrenaline that had carried her to this point was dwindling fast. She had to get out before he came after her.

A knock on the window made every cell in her body tense, thinking it could be Terrence. She instantly regretted the quick movement.

"Casey," Mrs. Harper called out, opening the door slowly. "You're in no condition to drive. Please, let me take you to the hospital."

At this point, she didn't have enough energy to fight, so she merely allowed the older woman to help her into the back seat before they drove away.

Taking shallow breaths, Casey tried to keep calm, but her husband's words echoed in her head and the emotional pain that struck her heart outweighed any physical pain.

"It was an accident ... "

"I never meant to hurt you ... "

* * *

When they arrived, Mrs. Harper guided Casey through the emergency room doors and to the patient registration desk. A security officer walked behind them, warning, "your car can't stay in the entrance zone."

"I'll be right back," Mrs. Harper said, turning to follow the burly man back in the direction they came.

"No, I'm here now," Casey protested. "You go on back to the Inn. I'll be alright."

Mrs. Harper moved the car and returned the keys to Casey. "I'll catch a taxi back to the Inn."

"Ma'am, what's the nature of your emergency?" a stone-faced intake nurse asked.

Casey chewed the inside of her jaw, tamping down an instant reply. She pulled the tan comforter tighter around her trembling body trying to ignore the curious stares of onlookers in the waiting room. A flamboyantly dressed woman with strawberry blonde hair eyed her carefully from a few feet away, while a couple holding a squirming toddler stared openly. No surprise when all of them inched back to give Casey some space.

"Wait … what did I do wrong?"

Her body, torn in a place where she warned him that she would never receive him, was racked with pain so severe that every step was pure agony. Blood had saturated the bottom half of the soft material wrapped around her body, but the worker had not looked up to gauge the situation. Instead, she had kept her sky-blue eyes focused on the computer while sliding a clipboard over the counter. What angered Casey the most was that the woman operated by habit, oblivious to the fact that she was the first point of contact for those coming into the hospital after suffering various injuries.

"Fill out this paperwork front and back," she said dryly. "Return it to me when you finish."

Feeling dismissed, Casey slid the clipboard from the ledge and cautiously maneuvered past those who averted their gazes. After a few minutes of being unable to find any stable position where the pain was not a constant enemy, or without the memory of why she was in this current state flashing in her mind, she realized standing at the counter would be best.

"Baby, believe me ... it was an accident."

The worker gestured in Casey's direction while speaking with another much taller woman on her right, but Casey was too far away to hear the conversation. She handed the clipboard over and watched as the woman keyed some information into a computer while the tall one hovered over her shoulder.

Infuriated by the disrespect, Casey let loose with, "Not once have you looked up from that screen to make eye contact with any of the people who are here."

Suddenly, a spike of tension hit the waiting room. Once again, all eyes focused on Casey.

"We're decent people," Casey said as another nurse snapped to attention and moved closer. "With real situations, who need just a little compassion. Obviously, you've been at this job so long that you're desensitized to the human aspect of your position." She leaned in, bracing against the counter so she could stay upright. "After everything I've been through this morning, having to deal with your callous attitude has been far more degrading."

When the woman still had not given her eye contact, Casey snapped, "Look at me."

Finally, she had the woman's full attention. "What's the nature of your emergency?"

Casey simply stared at her, waiting until the nurse's gaze lowered, doing a thorough onceover this time. Her blue eyes widened in shock. "You could've said that you've been raped," she whispered, and actually had the nerve to sound annoyed.

"It wasn't just rape," Casey said in a low voice. "It was something so despicable that I can't even say it out loud. The fact that I'm here should've been important enough no matter what happened to me." She finished in a voice loud enough for others to hear.

Grumbles of agreement from the waiting patients echoed behind Casey. Some even applauded.

The nurse flinched, then mumbled something to the other nurse that Casey could not quite catch. A more matronly woman walked over, placed a hand on the intake nurse's shoulder and said, "Why don't you take a break, Brenda. We'll talk later."

Brenda stood, grimaced, directed a stony gaze at Casey and said, "I apologize for your inconvenience," before trudging down a hallway that led to a double set of wooden doors.

"My name's Olivia," the older nurse offered, touching Casey's elbow. "I'll take over from here." Chestnut eyes, filled with warmth, flickered over Casey's ill-clad form as she added, "The police will catch the monster who did this."

"I'm sorry. I never meant for that to happen."

Casey's vision blurred with unshed tears as she whispered, "They won't have to look far. It's my husband …"

About the book

During an anniversary trip, Terrence, and Casey's marriage spirals into an unlikely abyss the moment he does the unthinkable. After eight years of occasional wedded bliss and with this violation weighing on them, Casey leaves the bedroom, then their home, and sets an immediate path towards freedom. Unfortunately, she soon finds out that the laws where the incident took place, and ones enacted where they live, are drastically different. Casey has a successful therapy practice, but now she's the one who needs counseling and a safe place on all fronts.

Desperate to repair his marriage, Terrence embarks on a painful expedition of self-discovery. With the tide of local laws blurring the lines of his actions, his path will lead him to challenge old ideas of women and his perceived rights of a man in marriage.

Can this couple find peace and a common ground when their definition of right and wrong are polar opposites?

"You think I chose Ahmad because he's handsome, wealthy, or because he's a person of color. No, it's because he makes me feel safe, and cared for, and cared about. And that was hours before we made it to this place."

She stood straight, with a fierceness she didn't feel and studied every face in the room. "I was here, looking for myself—some part of me that I lost—I didn't realize that doing the healing work restored the first part, but Ahmad is giving me the rest."

She pointed her finger at all of the men. "If you've ever, ever overruled a woman's no—and deep down you know that you have, realize you did the same thing to her, that those boys did to me. It didn't matter that I had consented to one of them, that didn't mean all of them could have a turn."

She grimaced at the pain the memories brought forth. "And who could I tell? I wasn't supposed to be there. I was supposed to go to the grocery store and come right back. I disobeyed my mother, so I deserved it, right? All these years, I thought that what they did to me was my fault for that reason alone."

"Honey." Ahmad pulled her trembling body against him.

"I'm here. I'm here." The hurt continued to pour from her lips as she locked a tear-filled gaze with the men who were the worst of the culprits.

"You're supposed to be our protectors and defenders. Our brothers, fathers, cousins. But who protects us from you? We can't even be safe in places that tell you how much we need to understand consent."

Tears streamed down her cheek. "I was so ashamed when Charli asked if we could hold a Bliss event, one geared to the Black Community. I broached the subject with a few of the guys that I play Bid Whist with. The idea of consent was so blurry, their intent so ugly, I knew I couldn't subject my sisters to that. They said, and I quote, 'Oh, I'm gonna get me some. Those men—men, I've known for years, and their response was to assert that they were going to get some ass before it was over. No different than those four boys." Her flawless pink nail pointed at each man who had come for her. "No different than you all here today. So I'm finding that this disregard isn't a Black or white thing. Rich or poor, even. It's all about that little piece of meat between your legs, and the brain attached to it believing life and death is in the power of its existence."

The ticking of the clock grew louder in the silence. "So don't get upset that I chose Ahmad. Try to figure out *why* I chose him." She traced Ahmad's muscular chest with one finger. "He is awesome. He is compassionate. He is intelligent. He is loyal. He is fine as hell, and most of all, he respects my boundaries and asks what I want to do." Her death stare made Oliver squirm. "You want it that bad, huh? You've been sex starved all your life—and must have me, right?" She waved her arm and stopped where each woman was situated. "When all these other women consented."

"But they're not you," Stewart said, bypassing the bodyguard and Oliver to move further into the room.

This asshole didn't hear a word I said. Alyssa shook her head and sank on the sofa. "You know what? Since you want to make this all about wet ass and slick dick. I'll save you from yourself. Be quick about it." She raised her white dress halfway up her thighs and smiled in an inviting way.

Chest heaving, Oliver glared at Ahmad for the longest time, then smirked and moved forward. But it was Stewart who brushed past him on his way to the sofa.

"I swear on everything I consider holy," Ahmad said through his teeth, but loud enough for it to echo through all the rooms. "You lay one finger on her, and I'll toss your ass over that fucking balcony."

Everyone froze. Oliver threw a panicked gaze at Ahmad and stepped back, quickly shoving his hand in his right pocket.

"And just know that when you were done," she said with a glare at Stewart. "I was going to need Ahmad—a real man—with some real dick, because I'm pretty sure you were about to give me some pussy."

Pin drop quiet was an accurate assessment of the lack of noise around them.

"And I'm pretty sure you're thinking that she has one of those already," Ahmad said to Stewart and Oliver, trying to keep his smile from taking over his face. "But I named hers … Heaven. And I promise you that it—and she—are divine."

"Damn that was cold," Charli said, grimacing along with a few other women before she said, "Every night you come in here packing wood, swearing you can hammer nails with it." She made of show of peering down at Stewart's crotch as she planted herself between the two men. "Right now, you're hanging so low you could stir coffee at the equator.

"That's if he had enough of one to begin with," Shelly chimed in, putting a stony glare on Stewart, who had turned several colors before landing on beet red.

"Enough! This is no laughing matter," Stewart roared, and everyone froze again.

Ahmad's gaze connected with Alyssa's. "Don't you ever do that again," he warned her, moving forward to take his rightful place beside her. "I know you didn't mean it. You didn't want it. You were testing their sense of decency. Baby, They. Have. None!"

"Permission to embrace you," Charli said.

"Yes."

Charli wrapped her arms so that Ahmad was sandwiched between them. Then another woman asked the same question. And yet another. Until every woman in the room surrounded Alyssa, holding her. They stayed that way for a while as she cried for that little girl who had been devalued in that way.

Ahmad's knuckles turned white from the force in his fist, probably with the need to smack one of them. "So, no, honey. I know how you meant it, but he was going to take you up on that offer. And I was going to need bail money." He pulled up her sleeve again to display the scar. While everyone else gasped, Ahmad leaned over and placed several kisses on that very spot. "This doesn't diminish your beauty. It shows me survival, persistence, and tenacity. It tells me you are loved by the Most High. Even though your heart is bruised and scarred, you're still here and that, my love, is beautiful."

"I will do my best to make sure you're always protected and safe—even from me."

About the book

Rahm Fosten did time for a crime he didn't commit. Now that he's free, taking care of the three women who supported him on a hellish journey is his priority, but old enemies are waiting in the shadows.

Rahm's dream life as a Knight of the Castle includes Marilyn Spears, who quiets the injustice of his rough past, but in his absence a new foe has infiltrated his family.

Marilyn Spears waited for many years to have someone like Rahm in her life. Now that he's home, an unexpected twist threatens to rip him away again. As much as she loves him, she's not willing to go where this new drama may lead.

Meanwhile, Rahm's gift to his Aunt Alyssa brings her to Durabia, where she catches the attention of wealthy surgeon, Ahmad Maharaj. Her attendance at a private Bliss event puts her under his watchful eye, but also in the crosshairs of the worst kind of enemy. Definitely the wrong timing for the rest of the challenges Rahm is facing.

Alex Williams sat on the passenger side of the patrol car watching the towering buildings of downtown Atlanta go by. His partner of five years, Maxwell Collins, drove with one beefy arm hanging out of the window. The balmy fall night air felt good blowing through the open windows.

They were two hours away from the end of an uneventful shift and Alex smiled. He would see her soon.

"What you so damn happy about, youngster?" Max asked.

Alex adjusted the seatbelt and turned to his friend. "When's too soon to get married?"

"Man, she got you wide open." Max laughed as he stopped at a red light.

"I'm serious," Alex said. "I'm ready to lock it down." He had never fallen this hard or this fast for a woman. Kelsee consumed his thoughts.

Max maneuvered through the intersection and scratched his head. "Speaking as someone with two ex-wives, a girlfriend and a friend with benefits, I say it's never too soon for love."

"Would you quit playing?" Alex said with a chuckle. "I'm making life decisions over here."

"Alright, alright." Max pulled into a gas station and cut off the engine. "Listen. Only you'll know if it's right. If you want my opinion, though, Kelsee's a nice girl."

Alex nodded. He valued his partner's input. They may have been total opposites – Max was white and divorced with three kids. Alex was a single, Black Muslim and almost twenty years his junior. But Alex knew he was ready. He was twenty-seven, advancing in a job he loved, and he had found his one.

He took a deep breath. "I'm going to do it."

Alex wondered what Kelsee was doing at this moment. They had plans to hook up when he got off work. He knew she would have something hot and ready for him and he wasn't thinking about food.

As soon as they returned to the car, the radio squawked, "Signal 58." Domestic violence call. The address was a familiar one in the Five Points neighborhood. They were a few blocks away, so Alex responded that they were on the way.

They screamed to a stop in front of the house and Alex was out of the car before Max could put it in park.

"I told Bob what would happen if we had to come back here," Alex yelled back at Max.

"Slow down, man. Follow procedure," Max instructed.

All Alex heard was the blood racing through his veins. The front door was ajar and before Alex hit the first step a half-dressed woman jumped out. She was followed closely by her husband.

Alex didn't think. He tackled Bob and started pounding him. Bob's face blurred and became someone else. With every punch, he rained down fury on his father.

"Are you trying to blow it?" Max asked him. They were back in the car outside the scene. "I had to pull you off the guy before you killed him."

"I warned him," Alex said watching the EMS workers put Bob on a stretcher. "I told him if we had to come here again it wouldn't be good for him."

Max opened the car door. "Don't worry about it. The guy was resisting arrest from what I saw. Besides, he was chasing his wife with a knife."

Alex massaged his bruised knuckles. He didn't even register the weapon when he attacked. That could have been a fatal error, but he didn't care. Alex couldn't explain what came over him.

Max exited the vehicle and talked to the other officers milling around the scene. Alex stayed put and nursed his anger. How could a man beat the woman he's supposed to love?

All he knew was the anger felt was as familiar as breathing. Alex took several deep breaths and was able to calm down. He would have to cancel on Kelsee tonight. She knew about his past, but he couldn't let her see the violence that coursed through his DNA.

About the book . . .

A tragic accident took the life of Kelsee's mother, whose dying words were, "Always save yourself first". She kept that in mind until she met a real-life hero, Officer Alex Williams. Their marriage wasn't a fairytale, but Kelsee hopes a child can save their union. But can the ultimate betrayal cause her to lose everything?

Alex regrets being unable to save his mother from an abusive relationship. He dives into a career that puts him in harm's way daily. Then he lays eyes on Kelsee and falls hard. Despite his family's disapproval, he sets out to make her his own. Can he live up to his "nice guy" persona or give in to the demons in his DNA?

The couple struggles to conceive, and when Kelsee really needs Alex, will he rescue her again or will she learn he is not that nice?

Chapter 1–Adrienne

I wish I could go back in time. Back to a time when I'm not sitting in an examination room waiting for the doctor to return and tell me what I already know to be true.

Closing my eyes to the harsh glare of fluorescent light, I shift on the exam table as the paper crinkles beneath me and blow out a stream of air. I tell myself I have this all wrong. Any number of things can cause a missed period. I have put off this visit for weeks, content to live in denial. Now, I cross my arms and wince. My tender breast ache and my stomach is queasy.

Three months into my marriage and I've already messed up. I will have to tell my husband. And Logan will not be pleased.

My stomach churns. I hop off the table and make it to the small restroom in two strides, kneeling in front of the toilet. While on my knees, I send up a prayer that my husband will accept this gift and forget about my reluctant agreement. Logan's demand to not have children almost doomed our marriage before it began, but I relented to his terms after weighing the option of being left alone again. Marrying a lawyer put me at a disadvantage in arguing a point.

I hear the *tap, tap* of someone knocking at the door. Dr. Taylor has returned with the results.

"Be right out," I yell as I flush the toilet. At the sink, I stare in the mirror before I wash my hands. I do not recognize the woman staring back. All my confidence is gone. I want to run, but my legs go weak and I grab the sink for support. *Get it together,* I tell myself. Being pregnant is not a death sentence. My marriage may end, but I've been through worst. I will my limbs to move and open the door.

When I walk back into the exam room, Dr. Taylor and his nurse are beaming. He presents the positive test to me. The plus sign marked in blue makes me ecstatic and terrified at the same time.

I think back to that Saturday a month before we were married. I had convinced Logan to accompany me to one of my student's soccer game. As a kindergarten teacher, I enjoy interacting with my students outside of the classroom. It helps me connect with the children and their parents. One of my favorite students, Keenan, told me about his soccer tournament and I had promised to be there.

Five minutes into the game, Logan leaned over. "Why did I agree to come to this again?"

"You didn't want to miss the "Tiny Titans" advance in the playoffs," I teased.

"No, I think you got me in a moment of weakness."

"What weakness? You were conscious."

"Maybe, but I believe you were naked at the time." His eyes warmed, and I knew he was reliving the memory of the night before and the shower that morning.

I elbowed him in the side. "Would you focus? I thought you might enjoy this. Didn't you used to play soccer?"

"A long time ago." Logan tucked the blanket around my legs. I liked the way he used any excuse to touch me.

"But you were good, right? Your mother said you had a soccer scholarship to college."

Logan sighed. "That's right, and then I buckled down and got serious. I left that childish game behind and concentrated on my studies. I had to get ready for law school."

Logan once told me his father never approved of the game. He was expected to follow in the family business and take over the law firm. I suspect there is more to that story and I started to ask him about it when I spotted my student.

"There he is," I pointed. "There's Keenan. Number 5."

We watched as a skinny sandy-haired boy streaked down the field with the ball rolling in front of his nimble feet. The kid was pretty good, considering most of his teammates were running in place, looking at someone on the sidelines or utterly clueless.

"Yes!" I jumped to my feet and clapped. "He scored. Way to go, Keenan!"

Keenan pumped his fist and did a dance. When he heard my voice, he looked toward the stands and blew a kiss.

I laughed and sat down. "I told you he's a mess."

"I thought teachers weren't supposed to have favorites," Logan said.

"We don't. Unless we do," I nudged him in the side.

Logan pulled me close. "What's up with you and this kid? Is he trying to take my girl?"

"Are you jealous, Mr. Rutherford?"

"No way. Besides, he is not old enough to do this." He turned my face to his and kissed me.

I remembered getting lost in the promise of that kiss. I was a lucky woman to have a man like Logan love me so completely. And then, my illusion of the perfect man disappeared in a single breath.

After the game, we exited the bleachers and went to meet Keenan and his parents. I kneeled for a hug from my student and stood to make introductions. We made small talk for a few minutes before the conversation turned to our upcoming wedding.

"I bet you guys can't wait to have children of your own," Keenan's mother said.

Before I could respond in the affirmative, Logan piped in. "That's not something we plan to do."

A pit formed in my stomach, but I held my questions until we were in the car. "What did you mean back there? Why would you say we aren't having children?"

Logan stared straight ahead and shrugged. "I meant what I said. I don't need to have any children."

We argued on the way home. I loved kids. That's why I became a teacher. I wanted the dream, marriage and two rugrats of my own. I pleaded with Logan, but he wouldn't budge. He lost all patience and said, "This is a non-negotiable item for me. I don't want any children. We aren't having any children."

When he saw the hurt on my face, his voice softened, but not his stance. "All I want is you. I'll give you everything, Adrienne. I love you and I want you to be my wife. We don't need children to be happy."

We discussed the issue for days, followed by bouts of strained silence with neither of us willing to concede. Then Logan threw down the final gauntlet. "The woman I marry needs to understand that there will be no children."

I realized I had to choose. But this positive test changes everything.

"When was the date of your last period?" Dr. Taylor repeats the question.

I struggle to remember. The wedding and honeymoon were a blur. Logan and I dated for five months before he proposed. We planned a wedding in a month. And now, we are about to be parents.

Based on the best guess of my last period, Dr. Taylor notates I am exactly twelve weeks along. He conducts an exam followed by an ultrasound to confirm the time frame. In six months, I will have a baby.

I leave the doctor's office with a prescription for folic acid, several pamphlets and the book, *What to Expect When You're Expecting*. Too bad there wasn't a manual to explain telling your stubborn husband we are expecting. I sit in the car, cell phone in hand and stomach in knots. I debate calling Logan at the office, instead my fingers punch in another familiar number.

"I'm on my way over."

"Well, hello to you too, Sister. Why aren't you at work?"

"I took the day off. Be there in a few." I pull out of the downtown parking garage and head for the interstate. The balmy fall day does nothing to bolster my sullen mood.

The best thing about living in Columbia, South Carolina, besides the mild winters, sweltering summers and Carolina college football games, is that you can get to almost any part of town in less than thirty minutes. Today, I make it to Kim's in fifteen.

Pulling into the driveway of my first major purchase after college always makes me smile, but not today. I want to celebrate my good news, but the thought of Logan's reaction tempers my attitude.

I have a key, but I ring the doorbell. Kim opens the door and I blurt out, "I'm pregnant."

"Oh. My. God," Kim screams, opening her arms to me. "I'm so happy for you."

I exhale and hug my sister. Everything will be okay now. Kim will help me make sense of things. I have always looked up to my little sister, literally. The woman is six feet tall without heels with a model-thin body. She has our father's height. I am six inches shorter with the curvaceous build of our mother.

I follow Kim through the house into her office, taking in the most recent decorations. I marvel that I once lived here. My sister's eclectic tastes are noticeable throughout the bungalow and reflect our differences in taste, especially her home office. The walls are painted a faux stone texture and complement the wicker fan back chair I am offered.

Kim slides behind her wrought iron glass-topped desk and clicks the mouse. "I'm on deadline for this website design." Her hair falls in ringlets around her shoulders as she works.

"Was Logan excited when you told him?" Focused on the computer screen, she doesn't see my pained expression.

"I haven't told him yet."

Kim stops typing and looks up. "Things haven't changed?"

I shake my head. "His decision is final on the subject. I couldn't change his mind."

"Men say that all the time, but they don't do anything to prevent it."

"That's true." Once we got married, Logan threw out his box of condoms in a symbolic nod to his commitment to our marriage.

"Then he should know that nothing is one hundred percent effective. No birth control is."

"Yeah, but he doesn't know I stopped taking the pill before we got married."

Kim leans back and frowns. "You know that's not cool."

"I know, I know. But I'm already thirty. I thought I would've been married a long time ago with at least two kids by now."

"Is that why you got married so quick? Because of Christopher?"

The mention of his name makes my heartbeat fast. The love I lost. "This isn't about Christopher."

"This is me you're talking to. It's always been about Christopher. I was there, remember? You dated the man for two years and then it was over. The way he ended it. Don't try to pretend he didn't hurt you."

"Okay, yeah. He hurt me." I concede the point. "But that's history. I think I'm over it now."

Kim shoots me a look and walks over to the printer. She exams her design and smiles. "If you say so. Anyway, Logan will get over himself and be fine. Or not. Either way, I'm going to be the coolest auntie."

I hang my head and groan. "What am I doing?"

"Don't beat yourself up. You know you'll be an excellent mother. You raised me and look how good I turned out," Kim says with a wink.

I smile. "I guess. You are kind of great."

"Thanks to you. I know what you gave up."

I wave my hand. We are not having that conversation again. "No one else would take care of a bratty thirteen-year-old. I was stuck with you."

Sometimes I wondered how either one of us turned out sane after dealing with so much grief. Mom died after a long illness, and we had adjusted to having lost her when Dad passed less than a year later. We lived with dad's brother, his wife, and our cousin until I turned eighteen. They were our relatives, but they made us feel like visitors. Visitors that had overstayed their welcome. I got us out of there as soon as possible. It's been Kim and me ever since.

"I wish they were here too," Kim says, picking up on my mood without me having to say a word.

"I miss them at times like this. They would be so excited to be grandparents."

I nod my head. "Yes, they would."

"Which Al Green song do you think Dad would play?"

Dad had Al Green's collection and would play the album every night.

Our lullaby was a soulful soundtrack about life and love. Kim leans over her laptop and clicks the mouse a few times. The strains of *Look What You Done for Me* sing from the computer speakers. "This is a celebration," she says. "Brother-in-law will come around."

We listen for a few minutes, chatting about due dates and possible baby names. Then the first notes of *How Can You Mend a Broken Heart?* start to play. Kim turns off the music but the vibe in the room changes.

"Every time I hear this song, I think of Dad playing it over and over after Mom died." Kim's voice breaks.

She reminds me of the scared little girl she used to be. I lean over the desk and squeeze her hand. She squeezes back and I walk around the desk to pull her into a hug. We take a moment to honor our shared history.

"You know what I think?" Kim sniffs.

"What?" I step away to grab a tissue.

"I think we should be celebrating. You are going to be a mommy." Kim does a dancing jig and boogies out of the room.

I follow her into the kitchen, wishing I could match her enthusiasm. I shiver and place a hand over my stomach. I hope Logan is ready for this because there is no turning back now.

I am keeping my baby.

About the book

When the cradle breaks the vows... all hell breaks loose.

Adrienne is obsessed with the new man in her life–the bouncing baby boy she's always dreamed of having... over her husband, Logan's staunch objections. Motherhood. Wealth. Power. On the surface, the joyful mother has it all – but beneath the bliss, a scandal is brewing that will rip her contentment to shreds.

Logan's professional aspirations leave little room for marriage, family...or guarding his secrets. He's laser focused on surpassing his father's success in the family law firm, and when an affluent new client breezes into town, Logan has one shot to overtake his father...if his wife will get out of his way.

When the past collides with the present, will the truth set Adrienne free?